Το Κοινόβιο

The Commune

Marios Chakkas

Translated by Chloe Tsolakoglou

Mercurial Editions, 2023

An imprint of Inpatient Press

TRANSLATOR'S PREFACE

Somewhere among the sun-scorched rocks, sloping hills, and the illuminated meadow in front of St. George's church, Marios Chakkas wrote: "All the times that I dreamt or hoped, I didn't delude myself; I only thought 'it is what it is, I missed my shot.'" And something else: I was forced to pay for dreaming; I was so blindsided that swore to never hope again." This word, *hope*, came to be the gilded arrow that pierced through Chakkas and in turn gave rise to *The Commune*. And, although he swore to never hope again, *The Commune* is strangely hopeful—or, rather, it is a work that reaches into the folds of both the past and future as to ignite the flames of a distant revolutionary dream.

From a young age, Chakkas' life was marred by various sociopolitical conflicts which required him to remain hopeful if he were to stay alive. Born in 1931 in Makrakomi, Fthiotida, he later moved with his family to the neighborhood Kesariani—a refugee quarter of Athens. In *The Commune,* Kesariani is a fundamental element of his personal mythology. This is where he experienced the tragic events of the Nazi Occupation and the Greek Civil War. In his teens, while he was studying in the Samaritan School of the Hellenic Red Cross, he voluntarily helped the prisoners in Gyaros and became involved in the leftist movements of Kesariani and Vyrona. On 30 April 1954, he was arrested due to his political beliefs and was sentenced to four years in jail;

it was during this time that he began to write fiction and plays. *The Commune* is the last book that Chakkas composed before he passed away at the age of forty-one due to cancer.

Though *The Commune* cannot be entirely designated as myth, it demonstrates Chakkas' world-building impulses through the use of poignantly exaggerated prose and a complete submission to language. He wanted to give language new dimensions—he grabbed ahold of the *is* of the thing, constellating the instants that composed his life. The result is a text which is highly ambiguous and idiosyncratic, subverting a coherent political ideal. This might seem counterintuitive considering the title of the book and Chakkas' own background. One might expect a detailed, linear narration of the commune, of the barracks, of his life as an insurrectionary.

But Chakkas did not write a memoir (or a personal mythology) that offered his reader consolation, a political manifesto, or a way for them to absolve themselves of the comings and goings of the world. He did not sensationalize his political experiences or his comrades' lives. Rather, he retreated into himself in a transformative process of unrestrained individuation. In *The Commune*, subjectivity rings forth in language until it acquires its own voice. The further away that Chakkas' commune may seem from a concrete, political reality, the closer it actually is to his revolutionary experience.

For Chakkas, the sociality of his work was to be communicated through his pathetic, messy reminiscence. Indeed, the words on the page are rushed and cataclysmic, like rain, like absolution. One of the only moments where the sociality of *The Commune* completely unmasks itself is in the last paragraph of the book. Chakkas noted: "There is a possibility that the name "[Kesariani] Shooting Range" will remain, but it will become neutral, it will not hold any significant meaning, it will be like Syntagma square, it will remind people of those loafers who shoot at paper targets, at clay plates and pigeons. They would never shoot at people. During the German occupation? When did such a thing ever happen?" The questions are obviously ironic.

On May 1st, 1944, two-hundred Greek communists were shot dead in Kesariani's shooting range as revenge for the death of a German lieutenant. The "200," as they came to be known, hold within them both the political dawn that has passed and the political dawn that is yet to come. It is in the ironic formulation of their deaths that Chakkas' name, the names of his comrades, the names of all of the insurrectionaries who have since been maimed, jailed, or killed by oppressive governments are whispered. The commune is on the horizon.

I dedicate this translation to all the incarcerated comrades across the world, including but not limited to: Christos Rodopoulos, Alfredo Cospito, Jessica Reznicek, Osman Evcan, Anna Beniamino, Eric King, Francisco Solar Domínguez, and others. I also dedicate it to those who have died, and those who persist, and those who could not imagine living any other way.

- Chloe Tsolakoglou

Το Κοινόβιο

The Commune

My writings are as small as bird droppings; on the second, maybe third page, they exhaust themselves, and then I dejectedly attempt to stretch them out, the sentences and innuendos like kittens which have been discarded at the dump. Sometimes I create arbitrary endings and I direct myself elsewhere. Other stories tangle themselves up inside of me, so I grasp the thread and I begin to unravel it, up until the moment it snaps again. Perhaps I seize it too abruptly. I leave my writings the way they birth themselves; fragments of a cleaved soul. To this day I cannot bring myself to write a longer piece, something akin to a chronicle.

I found myself at St. George the Koutalás, in a small meadow between Kesarianí and Karéa. If anyone were to ask me why I chose this piece of land to begin my novel, I naturally would not know how to answer. Let's say it was a kind of revelation. As I tugged this thread, I realized my writings were bound with steel wire—when I pulled them to the surface, the thread held. These sentences reflected each other, they lined up and marched forward.

From up here, I have a vantage point on life, the phrases readily pour down on me like a cataclysm, their meanings gleaming. This lasts for a while—days, months in heat, and I cannot bring myself tò do anything other than write, the typewriter's keys waste away, the ribbon deteriorates, the paper runs out though I have not yet begun, not even a centimeter of what's cluttered inside me is inscribed.

On this slice of earth all is illuminated. "Is it this simple?" I wonder to myself as I observe the brush scale up the mountainside, the hill beside me with the scorched rocks, the calcined tree which stubbornly holds itself up and the grove of eucalyptus trees—leaves dried from the pyre, and only at the hill's peak a tuft of green—attempting rebirth. The garden, too, with its tattered chrysanthemums bowing their heads to the ground, the grape vine superimposing its brilliant yellow leaves against the church's wall, the spring of water which runs softly alongside the cradle of the land; all of these things meld inside of me. I long to be a downcast chrysanthemum and lonesome tree, a eucalyptus whose sparse foliage sways in the wind, a vine that tries to find a home for its leaves. "This is who you are" I think, "the small, forgotten rivulet that wishes to exist."

For some, this space might not hold much meaning. A few years ago, even I preferred the park at Lombardiári, as I enjoyed the flora there, the way the crowns were dense—it is where I embraced women and even slithered my hand up their skirts; especially when dusk blankets the landscape, and the lights are dim, you can straddle a woman on top of you, light a cigarette, and drink your coffee all at the same time, and you know that just beyond the perimeter other couples revel in the same matters.

Such things tire me now. On one hand, you've got sickness, and on the other, old age, and most times neither of these have much merit, which is why I now avoid the spaces in which I once exhibited my pride. I prefer a bucolic walk at Koutalá and entertain the idea of appealing to the archdiocese in hopes of them delegating me this deserted meadow. Only a solitary nun resides here. They should assign her to some monastery where she'll be in the company of other crones, and a priest who will tend to the church—where she'll be an abbess who follows rules. What is she doing here alone?

I'll breathlessly trail alongside the hill's ridge to contemplate the scenery for my friends, the ones who are still standing, who have the courage to build an idiosyncratic commune.

My friend, the dentist, is sick of women now. He is a sturdy old man who does not disclose any inclination toward marriage. He is the most assured out of all of us. Sometimes he brings his tools up here with him and works free of charge for anyone willing to make the trip, which is a type of social reciprocity considering the openness of the land.

Panagákis, by exception, is the only married man here. In the old days, before his marriage, he thought about living a monastic life, and he traveled to ´Agion ´Oros[1], but I don't think that this yearning flame ever went out.. He is always longing for a morsel of well-cut bread and a comforting blanket.

Then there is Dimítris, who's been wrecked by women and alcohol. His hands shake vigorously, and he is unable to draw anymore. Perhaps he might be able to calm down again and pick up a brush, but it is unlikely considering his latest compulsions: He is obsessed with doubles; he takes his pills two by two, asks the waiter to cut his donuts in six, eight or twelve pieces. Always doubles. I know where this mania will drive him to: similar to the jailbird Stathoúros, who on most occasions was a sympathetic old man, but whose life was tortured by his obsession with pairs. He smoked his cigarettes two at a time and his deep inhalations also had to be twofold, and naturally, he had to reach fifty puffs on each cigarette (*fifty on this one*, he'd holler in the prison yard). It was the magic number; everything else in his life was coupled in twos. "The sun" people would tell him, "and the moon" he'd retort with emphasis. He then reached the point of pinching two clothespins on each of his garments, doubled the suds, and even started to count his steps, causing him to vomit all over himself. He did not converse with anyone out of fear of messing up his counting, and if people confused him, he muttered "go take a

---

1. Translator's note: This is a famous monastery in Greece where Orthodox monasticism is practiced. No women are allowed on the premises.

long walk off a short pier, you old bastards". He yelled all night and kept everyone awake in their cells. Even if Dimítris has this manic predisposition, we will consider not excluding him from accompanying us to the commune.

Tímos relied on his eyes and headed for foreign lands. First, he embarked on his journey as an undergraduate, but now who knows how he makes do. One thing is for certain, he does not work. His constant aporia is why people toil away at jobs and why soldiers lace up their boots, and for this people call him slow, but he does not pay them any mind. He stretches out in his tent and takes long naps.

Lest I forget Tsaoúsis. The sad sack wasn't even a sergeant. But he did care a whole lot about his tent and whether or not it would collapse from the winds and rain. His nickname stuck because he was the one who'd repair it and peg the stakes into the ground. Tsaoúsis was necessary for order. When our rooms begin to smell putrid, around six months' time, he'll grab us by our ankles and scold us, and he might even put one of us to work as the custodian.

This is not to say that we will have a person in charge, leader, or representative though. So many years we've been filled to the brim with wardens, chiefs, lieutenants, and all kinds of different authority figures; dicks who demanded that we all piss in unison at the urinals. (Your piss had to lap against the left side of the can; if it strayed away, you became a suspect). Good riddance. And what kind of people were we, then, to accept that treatment for so many years? It befuddles me to think that there are still individuals who willingly accept the rules of such a rigid life. What happens to them, and they choose to enlist? I, however, and my friends as far as I know, will never find ourselves in any kind of structure. If it concerns a literary association, secretaries, a president, and priesthood, we will have nothing to do with it. We don't have time to just try things out, and anyway, why would we attempt to traverse a road we know will lead us nowhere? Is it perhaps that the representatives were at fault and the authorities remain unscathed? This mess needs to be cleared up—authorities and representatives, form and content, ideas and praxis, they're all the same, and when you try to single one of them out, you're only trying to save scraps. So, the sum of all parts is at fault in this situation, leaders and members, hierarchy and committees, church doctrine and morons who resign to saying, "I believe." I believe nothing anymore—they're all clowns who need to be tossed out.

If people decide to build communes in the future, even if they're on the moon, they need to keep in mind that it would be best practice to round up all the good-for-nothing leaders and dump them in a crater. There, they can accrue dust, rocks, and dirt and build a new party if they wish. There is no way that we will willingly participate anymore, to put it simply. If, however, they corner us, then we will cede—what else can we do? We won't be thinking of the struggles at Marathóna, or the Gorgopótamo village. We'll only have this weathered hillside on our minds, with its laurel bushes, and the thought of our hands on women's limber bodies, or the way we'll play hooky on our way back to the house with the fer forgé chairs that need another layer of white paint—yes, these will be the things we'll reminisce on. As far as the "crusades" are concerned, they needn't worry; we're through with those kinds of tricks. Ideas have become half-baked now, and mischief and heroes have long since dwindled.

And, if all things considered, we need some type of government, then make some mother in charge of the Ministry of Birth, make a twenty-something year old stud responsible for the Ministry of Eros, and delegate the Ministry of Death to an old pensioner. These ministries would suffice. There are lackeys with their bureaucratic filing cabinets, and others without, but who all project their insecurities onto us and demand that we consider them our saviors. Isn't that something. No one can save us, and this is something that the Minister of Death knows; he sees this despair every day in the gallery of corpses—one, two, three—so many perish, no one is salvaged. Therefore, the Minister does not boast. He does a typical job, counting the dead; he is cognizant of his fate and does not have an appetite for more power.

The young man, Minister of Eros, supervises the hotels

and ensures that they have wonderful presentations and pleasant music—not at all like our time spent in decrepit banquet halls with cracked speakers and a hotelier who remotely changes the radio stations according to his whims. And like this, in the most critical moments, I happened to tune in to directions aimed at sailors, news about thousands of dead people, wars, typhoons, and the mawkish messages of German workers. Our rooms were only partitioned by thin drywall, so you could even hear your neighbor's labored breath—who knows how many holes were in the walls and how many eyes were surveilling you. And people wonder why we are the way we are. Even so, we're quite decent. We could be a lot more degenerate.

The twenty-something year old expands his supervision to the parks: "Here," he says, "we should place a queen-sized bed with a view of the pond. This is where the grass will be utilized." All around him there are employees taking notes, all young men who very well know what it's like to hold a girl in their arms.

Everything will be nice and dandy, at least for the young. No system or futuristic community can serve the old. They will have to face the great conqueror, the Minister of Death. I already look him in the eyes and feel that many times he is smiling at me, and so I am desensitizing myself to any inkling of hope.

All the times that I dreamt or hoped, I didn't delude myself; I only thought "it is what it is, I missed my shot." And something else: I was forced to pay for dreaming; I was so blindsided that I swore to never hope again. It was like the time I had a date with a woman I desired deeply. I went to meet her with my shoulders back and my chin held high. That same night I urinated blood. Following this, I haven't dared to keep my shoulders back or hold my chin up. I wander around reservedly and with a hunched back, I exist modestly and discreetly, if possible, even if it is difficult to ultimately disappear from people's memories. The Minister has taken note of my circumstance and is patiently waiting. I've been marked.

If there had been a mother assigned to the Ministry of Birth from the get-go, maybe things would be better. She'd care about the way I carry myself, and she'd make sure that I am in constant contact with the world. Completely unlike what happened to me: They cut me at my navel. They knotted up my umbilical cord so I could never aspire to form a new connection. I was in pain and began to sob about not being able to have a direct bond with the world. Since then, I plummet absent-mindedly onto sweaty sheets, and my life has become the anxiety of falling.

I was falling, always falling in relation to some distant star. I charted an elliptical orbit and at the end found myself landing on the dirt, maybe even wedging myself into a grave. I was cheated. "You can't resolve your problems with a general and abstract descent," the stars flickered—a sign of danger. I navigated around the rocks a little too closely, so much so that my pants tore up. "Maybe on the other trip," I thought to myself and adjusted my direction with the purpose of discovering a connection to other galaxies, somewhere that I can grab onto and rescue myself from this chaos.

The best period of my life was when I tumbled into that tepid stream of air—something like a Gulf Stream—when I met the girl with warm feet. For the first time, I didn't have to heat up a woman's legs in bed. This created an urge within me that made me want to dance, to float about. It did not last long. The people who prepared the weather report predicted cold wind and I began to have reservations. I was falling again, but not solely as a result of my body's weight, which is very natural, but also due to other powers who were plotting and fabricating an endless void beneath me. I only realized this because I had a gut feeling, and my ganglia swelled up—it is not easy to discern if you are falling when in motion. Everything around you jumbles; people, ideas, and the universe, and all the while you think that it's all normal.

And like this, I fell straight onto my back in a general direction; I saw Mr. Masturbation standing there with all his belongings strewn about, his knapsacks strapped to his back and a sycamore leaf covering his junk. He was wearing a coat and naturally had his hand in his pocket. With the park as a backdrop, Mr. Masturbation smiled idiotically while observing the ongoing traffic. Happy Mr. Masturbation. I got up and walked along and thought of Mr. Eftíchios[2]. How does this all cancel out? How does he come into play? Why is his trench coat buttoned up the wrong way? How is his sycamore leaf staying put with all this wind? I noticed that he, too, was severed and that his umbilical cord was non-existent, and his puppet strings were attached to a distant purpose. His only connection was to himself. This is when I understood, when I realized: Under his coat, he was stroking the only cord he had left; his intestine. It was hanging there. This is what they had allowed him to keep, and it was a wonderful way to communicate with the world. He did not need to hold on to anything else because everything had come full circle.

Why do I bother with trying to communicate with other people? What does the commune need now? Why don't I act like every Mr. Masturbation or Mr. Eftíchios? Why do I lose myself in my writing? It's all about me and my little car. Me and my little shop. Me and my house. So many things are in my periphery, I do not need to create connections with other people. If possible, I would like to avoid wandering around this morose landscape any longer.

Come on, you bastard, write about normal people—the ones you walk past, even for just a second, the ones who made

2. Translator's note: This name means "good luck" and is typically associated with happiness.

impressions on you. Write about what it is like to live in the yard, the jail cells and barracks, or the man who used to sit on a stool and teach his friend how to play the bouzouki.

But of course, there was no bouzouki. All of the musical beginnings, variations, and endings were instead played by people's mouths and hands. Those are the ones who keep the score.

The lyric "Cry a little bit so I can get off the hook" was playing, and I suddenly remembered how they advised Socrates to drag his wife, Xanthíppe, and their kids to the courts so that they could weep and put on a good show.

"If you're a mother who's hurting," was the following verse, and I thought of Halil Bey's mother[3], how she stood in front of "the armies of Moreá[4]" after the great catastrophe, crying about her son alongside Xerxes' mother. The cries of victorious joy were not audible, only the loser's wails of sorrow marked the air. It was that universal sobbing.

My teacher, I hope that you're still waiting around at your post on that weathered stool, teaching the age-old cries of pain, even if the bouzouki[5] has been taken away from you. The

---

3. Translator's note: Halil Bey was a military commander in the region of Lamia during the Greek War of Independence.

4. Translator's note: Name given to the Peloponnese peninsula in southern Greece. It is considered to be the backbone of the Greek Revolution.

5. Translator's note: Popular music instrument used in Greece. It belongs to the lute

method does not matter. If you have meráki[6], expression will pour out of you. Transform your tongue into a pick and play whatever lights you on fire; the heat alone will reignite the embers of 1821[7]. You'll even reach further than that historic revolution, all the way back into Socrates' time, and perhaps beyond that, too. You might find yourself at Hecuba's lament.

Everything exists inside of me, and this is why I sing for my friends, why I am designing a commune that is not subject to the world's social impositions. The hillside's obituaries, its psalms of wounds caused by the stone quarries, and the castrated pine trees will jolt us out of our worldly loneliness.

When I howl in Koutalás canyon, my voice ricochets off the rocks and comes back to me. When I shout from an apartment's lightless room, my voice sinks into the foam of many couches. When I yell from my dream's deep well, my voice gets caught between my clenched teeth and slides back down into my entrails, coloring them black.

I will write about the sleepless nights of old boy Pag-

family.

6. Translator's note: Common Greek expression that indicates putting something of yourself in your work. In other words, it means to create something with love, creativity, and soul.

7. Translator's note: This is a reference to the Greek War of Independence. With the assistance of other empires at the time, such as the British and French, the Greeks were able to liberate themselves from Ottoman rule.

gourélias.

He'd sketch on vellum all night and in the morning he'd show us a boat; it was the same every time. During the day, he'd erase all the sea foam, the sails, masts, and the anchor—this is why he would draw on vellum, because it was easy to erase the work. When dusk arrived, he would begin sketching as the street lights flickered on, or he would roll up mounds of thread. This is the way he spent his evenings on his little cot.

Once, I saw him clipping his nails—he cut them close to the nail bed to rid himself of rheumatism. He dug the clippers deep into his skin, hoping to mollify his aches. He thought, in doing this, that pain would flow out of his mangled fingertips.

One morning, we found his thread so well rolled that you could not find its beginning or end, and his vellum had an image of a different ship (it did not have an anchor, and its sails were dark, its masts were broken, and the sea was swallowing it whole). Old Paggourélia was curled up on his cot, looking at his nails. He'd finally been able to cast out his rheumatism but with it went his last breath.

Another morning, I found myself walking around the meadow in Koutalá—it's not far away, only about a fifteen-minute walk from the last homes on the hillside—and I began describing how you'd be able to reach this place, and all the trees you'd see. I talked about the scorched slope, the dirt road leading to Kesarianí, and the other one that ends up at the stone quarry. There was the little church, too, which was always locked up, but its doors would open once the elderly nun realized that people were visiting. She hoped that they'd make some donations or purchase candles. It's very dark in there, and the antiquated iconographies are barely distinguishable underneath the layer of asbestos. There are two icons, lithographs of St. George—the classic images of him wielding the spear, the beast, and his horse standing on its hind legs.

He was a poor saint, without much acclaim, and was usually depicted with a spoon in hand, hence the name St. George the Koutalás. The nun believes that he crafted spoons to sustain himself. But, of course, the name could also originate from elsewhere or be metaphorical. I suddenly remember Mrs. Bébi, and her son, who in making an offering to the Saint would utter "here you go, poutána." Mrs. Bébi would be quick to correct her son's supposed mistake, and she'd explain that he did not mean to call anyone a whore and would retort: "He meant to say Koutalá, he said Koutalá." This confused the skeptical bystanders, herself, and her son, who then blurted out: "Here you go, Koutalá."

This is exactly it: the Saint lived a horny life. Though, I don't think he was a pervert. This presupposes traveling by buses and trolleys, which did not exist in his time. I am disgusted by such things. These guys extend their arms and hands and try to grab anything; asses, backs, and sometimes when there's little space, they even feel up the men. After doing so, they satisfy themselves and continue their fantasies. Neither do I believe that St. George got off when people came to confession, because women are too modest and want to avoid scandals. What I believe is that he was a downright womanizer, but ultimately became tired of the game and resigned to this little crack in the mountain and wrote about his experiences. Maybe he even concealed them behind psalms or other religious stories and made spoons here and there during his studies.

Either way, I think we are quite similar. I am also tired of women, and I own a shop filled with my own handmade items, which is kind of the same thing. These analogies, alongside this idea I have to write a novel, highlight the similarities between us. Memories of the times when I was rebellious, of when I was young and excited by some ideas, relationships that beautified my life, and the way that these ideas and relationships ultimately died, the way that my youth went to waste, my friends—some in the looney bin and others in their graves—all of these bring me closer to the Saint. They make him solely mine.

This is how I think that he slowly lost his marbles, too. If you act crazy for more than a week, then you're a goner and you will lose your friends. If you are someone who does not forget their umbrella on the bus, you are a regular person and you do not belong with my group of people. We might not have been able to achieve great things in life, but we created fulfilling friendships. We all lost our marbles, but we didn't pay any mind. The idea for the commune began like so: We need a place to assemble because we can't get enough of each other.

The one guy who did not care about ever getting enough of his friends was Phaedon, who was in some way in charge of our Wednesday meetings. He said "As long as I am able to write poems, I could do without friends. When I stop writing, loneliness chokes me." He hadn't been able to scribble a single stanza in six months and decided to go to the doctor's office every Wednesday. Someone was going to make a comment about creating a program and how it isn't right to have this habit, and Phaedon simply glared at him until he stopped talking. On Wednesday, he made himself comfortable on the couch, sat between the different clients, and waited. The doctor, standing at the door between the couch and the office, saw Phaedon there and instead of asking "Whose turn is it?" like he normally would, declared that he was tired and that he would not take any more patients that day. They remained there, looking at each other. This was the first Wednesday in my friend group's history.

So, we slowly started to convene and about ten of us would talk about art, even though we didn't really think that this was the topic that united us. We argued like normal people, we all piled on top of a scapegoat and ragged on them to the point of elimination, and we never agreed on anything. This is the reason why we were not even able to put out a single magazine; we always stumbled over literary miseries. We were little people who quarreled over the order of the texts, where we'd place our names and in what style, if it'd be typeset in Elzevir or something simpler.

It was actually quite nice, though, to be able to lean on one another in that small doctor's office. We maintained a commune that was beyond art. Especially when our conversation turned over to our teenage years and we talked about going to the brothels and how one of us almost got married at the height of his horniness. During these moments, a wave of warmth unfolded between us, and we were committed to one another; neither a tavérna nor any other hangout spot could have such an effect on our hearts.

At least we were all a team and we finally had what was withheld from us all these years. In the past, whenever we'd try to get together, they'd always catch us in the act and would toss us back onto the rocks. Every time we said that we wanted to believe in something, it immediately became air—or, other people made it so. It disappeared like the soap bubbles which popped between our hands. There was no vision left to hold on to and we became desolate.

St. George, my Koutalá and protector, please ensure that I

will finish these pages. I don't know how many yet. Maybe as long as I think I have something to say, even if I can't articulate it at the moment. You know that I'm no trickster, that I don't hit the ball out of the field just to delay the game. I am earnest in my endeavor to describe the lives of my saintly friends, the ones who used to be rocks but are now sponges. Even one of your own friends, St. Peter, was able to make amends and revive, regardless of his wrongdoings. My friends are also repentant, but they do not have the strength to recuperate, though they have the desire to believe in something. They're naively looking for it, looking for a way to hold on even though everything around us has deteriorated.

Even the stars have become unstable now that every evening collapses onto itself. There is nothing left to do but to cry alongside the incandescent stones that are slowly dying out—they will never again have the chance to travel across the stygian sky. How can my friends possibly hold when lately black spots have been punctuating the sun?

These kinds of people are my friends.

Phaedon had a horrendous ending; he became a public servant and was even promoted. Tsaoúsis' was even worse—he got married. Nótis is now expecting a child. The only ones left standing are Górpas, who is completely decimated, the dentist with his maladies, and two or three others who insist on writing. How long will they last? One by one we slink away and leave nothing behind, not even the trail that a slug would in its languid movement. This is how everyone comes and goes, and our Wednesdays have become an obituary column for those who remain.

Gerásimos is traveling the seas of China and has metamorphosed into a radio wave aimed at sending incoherent signals to Che. We've gotten old, Gerásimos. And, Thanásis, you've mortally wounded yourself. Thanásis, what are you trying to do. Why are you scratching at your scabs—this is not a solution, it simply isn't.

I was sitting underneath some weathered tamarisk trees. The sea was in front of me, and just beyond its edge, he was lying there dead. Some of our pals thought that he was resting comfortably, and others believed that he was in deep sleep and that he'd wake up soon. The sea, though, which was thrashing itself against the shore, and the tamarisk trees that spread their blossoms, knew. His sloping skull framed that familiar landscape; it had the same origin as the surrounding mountains. And his face was long and slender, his nostrils slightly curved. His upper lip was a small mountainside, and next to it there was a sudden ravine that kept his mouth ajar. The jaw and ears were not visible because they were obscured by the cape; a decadent casket which sealed him in. Beyond it, however, where the sea opened, you could make out the distant tips of his shoes. The mound, somewhere in the middle, was actually his tied-up hands. As far as memorial candles are concerned, you could spot them where you'd typically find a man's genitals—they were the telephone poles that embedded themselves in the arching landscape.

The peak of his head was bald, his face was carved up. Right above him there was a permanent cloud—a plume of frankincense—that frayed as it reached his nostrils. This same cloud cast a shadow to the right of him; it might've been raining there.

If you peered over the edge of the cape's casket, you could distinguish how there were deep plow marks on his chest; sage seeded there, as well as wild tea and mountain songs. Vineyards and olive trees were sprawled out on his stomach, and on his thighs, there were greenhouses. Down by his calves, the cape was bare and craggy.

Where his feet rested in the pelagic waters there was a rock that served as his small navigation boat. You had to guess its appearance due to the abundance of seafoam. It led him out to the deep sea for his final descent.

I still don't understand how a mountain can die. It is not due to the lacerations on his ribcage inflicted by the stone quarries, neither is it because of the lumber mills. He still has the capability to germinate tall trees and forests. It might be the fact that he was pursuing death. He probably lived through everything and decided to try something new.

He's traveling with his shoulders bent.

If he were alive, he'd stand up above the clouds, and with one leap, which of course would be quite big and difficult, he'd land on the island of Milos. There, everything would be easier. Carefully stepping over the clusters of islands, he'd cause an earthquake in Thíra and one of the nearby islets would submerge, and perhaps another would be born. He would then head for the necklace of the Cyclades, the North Sporades, and then a helpful wind would tug him even further north—it would make him travel, always travel.

Now, still bent, he is voyaging in the cyan water. He took cyanide. No commune is claiming his heart or sperm. He unshackled himself from society, from everything that is normal and regular.

We also lost Neophyte. "When will the halcyon days arrive, Thanási?" he'd ask while turning onto his stomach on the sand at the sunny beach in Fáliro. "Now?" the other would answer, "those days are long gone. It's February." And after a week had passed, he would ask the same: "When will the halcyon days arrive, Thanási?"

He never made it, never was able to see them, never tasted them. Still, he expired on an ordinary winter day—his heart gave out as he was swimming in the deep ocean, and the kingfishers, having watched him float from afar, mistook his large abdomen for a little island. They flew toward him to nestle their eggs.

Wake up, Neophyte. The days you were expecting have now arrived. Joyful kingfishers are escorting you to your final big race, they're supervising you and keeping time, they're encouraging you, and this time you will break the record. You'll come in first in front of the judges. Little laurels are waiting for you and people will hoist you up on their shoulders, they'll throw big celebrations and sing your praises.

The first gesture I remember making in my life was trying to unclasp my hand from another's. I must have been successful because even now I am flooded with the memory of running toward the "vaporáki," a big machine, which was a type of highway roller that happened to be setting tar at the time. The other's hand quickly grasped mine again and I received a good beating. This is the image that illustrates the beginning of my life: it is an effort for liberation, and subsequently, its consequence.

Only when I reached thirty-five years of age was I able to free myself from my constraints, and not fully at that. It is not easy to rid yourself of the burden of a political party. I always felt that they were holding my hand. Every time I tried to pull away, I paid a price, faced repercussions, isolation, and temporary citations. I was ultimately able to secede. My hand is unclasped and I use it however I like—whether it be giving someone the bird from between my legs or scratching my balls—I don't owe anything to anyone.

This is what I believe, though I am not sure about anything. My hand might be fastened elsewhere and my whole life is spent trying to pry it open, perhaps motivated by my anxiety concerning time, and how I can release myself from it. It's not a social issue that I can just shit on—as I realize the scale of the problem, I will become increasingly panicked. Then there's the issue of the escalators, which is quite like the aforementioned one. I started boarding them the wrong way. I always pursued difficult circumstances, and when our schoolteacher assigned us essays, I wrote very differently from everyone else. I recorded weird thoughts and fantasies whilst others followed an expected path. When I was younger, I achieved some milestones that were set against the normal way of things. Now that I'm heavy, I'm continually losing thoughts and I am witnessing my goals distance themselves from me. I walk backwards through the same markers and I likely end up further from where I had originally started. I will find myself at rock bottom. And all this is attributable to me not taking the escalator that went up. Obviously, I wanted to come off as a contrarian, but as the situation has it, I am not that—not that at all.

The social issues weren't for me, either, even though I got tangled up in them. There was a time in which I was able to free my grip on them; the truth is that they're kind of looming. I should have been a little less naïve, there is no excuse for me to reach thirty-five years old and excuse myself from this commune as well.

I recall there was a female worker in a condom factory that was located around St. Cocksburg. She was part of some Committee Association and protesting on behalf of Greece. Undoubtedly, she had no idea where to find our country on a map. I decided to sign a petition for Cameroon, and I was very troubled by the Kurds' problems. So, I became an internationalist and removed myself from the piteous Kesarianí. The Kurds certainly wear djellabas and might even sport turbans. The citizens of Kesarianí wear jackets and slacks and they're bareheaded. I like the Kurds' attire, especially when they're atop their horses. The people of Kesarianí don't have horses, not even their bakers—they've resigned to riding vespas around.

And the girl who is protesting (for lyublyu Gretsiyu—doesn't that "lyublyu" sound like the word bubble?), poor thing, is not at fault for anything—she might even be blond with braids and very likable. Nevertheless, her boss Bitchyniev (I can't quite remember what his name is) may decide to be the bigwig and will not relent.

There are plenty who would still say that this is the right way, or is what's appropriate, and so for them "everything has gone the best possible way." I don't doubt that this is the right way for them, even for the others who reside there, but I wonder what kind of collaterals I'm holding in my arms that apply to those who live outside of what's proper. I am primarily thinking about people like us, or at least myself.

Like this, the Bubblegirl stands for Greece, and I stand for Cameroon and the Kurds. Oh the Kurds, the poor Kurds—I have to care about them before they're all slaughtered. And Britchyniev (I can never remember the correct spelling) will play dead. I'll tell a friend of mine to keep the Estonians and Armenians in his thoughts because they always get the short end of the stick. Then we'll see if that makes a good impression on Krichyniev.

These are the worldly problems that caused nagging in the first place. There is no way I can care about Armenians, Estonians, Kurds, Asians, Africans, blue, and green people all at once. And to top everything off, there's Kesarianí. Put the demotic council to work and ensure that they come up with a voting outcome for Mali, motivate Mrs. Fenáki of F.E.N, M.E.N, and D.E.N. I don't have time to catch up with every local matter, and more, global issues weigh heavily on me—even if no one asks me about them. I send memorandums to Dritchyniev (I only get the ending right. Why the hell did they put him in charge if he has such a difficult name?) and I unsurprisingly receive no answer. I am persistent, nevertheless, and I ask the mayor "what is going to happen with the committees? Are they ever going to function? What kind of Commission Union are we?" Strichyniev (he's gone now, there is no way I'll run into him) focuses on other matters. They're trying to shut me up and ask, "why do you talk like that?" tell me "this is not allowed," "this is not right." You all can go to hell if you think that I'll give you a reason as to why I speak this way. I give monologues, either interior or exterior, however I like. Do you know how many years I spent listening to your egregious or apologetic monologues? Until I die, we will never be even. You really thought that you wouldn't have to pay up for all of the things you made me listen to during your propositions, and the fact that you only gave me five minutes to make an address which you then shut down by citing that you were "closing" for the day out of fear of me misinterpreting your reasoning. And really, I'm not even cussing him out, I just can't remember his exact name. I only began talking about the other matters in my own way and following my own truth in case I'm able to benefit the movement. Little by little I came to be where I'm currently at. I sometimes consider going further along and to stop caring about anything—to stop thinking of the Kurds, whom I love on any other occasion. I must stop caring because you've filled us to the brim with bubbles—the giants we used to be in awe of all these years are little people like you and me. In fact, their kind is genetically short and many of them had bowed legs. As far as their goalie is concerned, don't think that he simply stands still in the middle of the posts and extends his arms toward either corner to block the ball. He pulls many maneuvers and catches a good number of goals.

There is no way I am going to deal with regular issues again; I will only contend with regular women, if they want me. Obviously, we must still maintain some kind of government, but a ridiculous one so that I can mock it. We can't allow them to be sticklers as it will be much harder to extricate yourself from their business, and harder still to convince your friends that they're all one and the same. It doesn't matter how they appear, or if they speak beautifully, because a government is still a government. Fuck them and leave them to rot.

There is only one circumstance that will make me return to this commune: I need to take this issue seriously, I need to fight and then fall in dire moments. I cannot accept a government comprised of Greeks who are lackeys of the German state. Mockery is not enough for me. I want to slice it up and be put in charge of a firing squad where I'll be able to say "fire." It's all because I saw beards and flags swaying in the wind. I have also touched bandoliers and people's hopes. It was then, it was then, it was then that the slovenly citizens of Kesarianí closed down the hookah lounges and guarded all entrances to the neighborhood and wouldn't allow a single member of the Security Battalion to pass through. Unfortunately, I was still young at the time and was not given the opportunity to hold a rifle.

"Oh, if only the movement would hang on a little longer... Since your departure we've been decimated..."

I know many people who wasted their lives pursuing a similar political outburst. It was futile. Those days were the last thunder of a storm that has long since passed. It's raining elsewhere now. Some thought that the storm cloud would come back. The leaders even called in a rainmaker who would ensure its return. Ultimately, the group's fervor never recurred—but this was expected. On one side we've got the leaders, and on the other we've got the foreigners; this issue has been driven into the ground, and we've lost our chance forever. Only a memory remains, a continual elegy for those who were killed, for the youth that was lived with no fruitful outcome.

How did the nostalgia of reminiscence win me over? Why am I submitting myself to the cycle of repetition? In the end, it's not a question of my generation, since I was a child at the time that others were fighting in the war. I was only an afterthought in the whole debacle and could easily avoid it. So, what was I trying to do—trying to achieve in a situation with a predetermined outcome? Now I stand in front of an envelope containing all my youth; how can I refuse it. "Do something," they tell me, "about your weight," but I am not thinking of that kind of weight, I am thinking of another that will never lessen—it will instead increase as time passes. What else am I supposed to do? They need to understand that I don't have any correlation with those things. It is not difficult for me to draft up a memorandum, but it's hard to give up my friend groups—those same friends that I've known for the last twenty years. Giving them up would be impossible.

For twenty years I've slipped another piece of paper into the folder of my youth and watched it expand like a book in my hands. Every page a catalogue of smart-ass remarks, silliness, rebellious behavior and lies. And at the end, you realize that this is your book, whether the life you led was good or not. How could you possibly erase it or start over again? This is not to say that there isn't a threshold for fresh beginnings—even though I didn't have any. I wasn't able to lessen any weight and I know I will never be able to be twenty again; this is for certain. I don't even know if I would choose to start over again because the possibility of leaving socialism is slim when you grow up in Kesarianí during the German Occupation and you've got a tremendous hatred for paramilitarism.

For entirely personal reasons I found myself laying against the base of a tree. It was coiffed in a way that made it seem like it was flipping off the low clouds which were softening its bark and rotting its roots. I decided to make the same gesture with my arms and legs. I got bored rather quickly because there was no purpose, and I didn't try to expel the gas that was snaking its way around my stomach, either. The snake must have arrived now. They probably opened it, saw that it was full, and closed it back up again. Should I yell? If I do, the ganglia in my neck will swell and probably burst. "St. George," I whisper, "I'm reaching my end." I've said all that I need to about them, about you, and myself. I couldn't reside in any commune because I am unwanted, and I complained a lot. Therefore, with every page I wrote, my lungs, stomach, and liver bloated. Every phrase and paragraph were cancers. As long as my brain remains unscathed, I think I will be able to produce an occasional gem. The story about the woman and her chickens. I've mentioned those thoughts before and I understand that these are not the final moments.

I should hug the tree to hoist myself up. Its trunk is frozen and remains vertical. I always end up horizontal. I am going to keep this position until my blood drains. It will be milky because I have many white blood cells. White as the coming dawn, the eggshell, the mountainous fog. Nah, it's more like sperm. I prefer not to readjust myself. I am touching something cold.

The nun is sleeping. The coming shock will be more than enough for her. She's going to find me here, resting motionless underneath the tree. If I reluctantly impose myself onto her, nothing will happen because it is not my true desire. My mind will cease right below this tree. Any attempt of help should not be recorded. Alright, I've lingered enough; I can't lounge until the last minute. This is what people will think: they found him unconscious. The elevator stopped working and they lugged the stretcher up the stairs. They cut it too close on a turn and he said "Ouch." His friends were there for him. Based on the amount of plastic containers, you could tell that he ate a lot of yogurt, and maybe he died from the preservatives they put in food and frozen meals. What is a human? There is only one road: It begins with life and ends in death. Where does this path lead? Possibly to the mountain. I walked along it—it winds up nowhere, it loses itself.

At the last moment maybe my Saint will appear and be there for me. If I was ever a bad or unworthy man, he himself would use his spear or a rusty knife with sharpened edges—like how we used to fashion them in jail—to splay open my veins. If I was ever a fair man, he would cradle my head and utter words of sympathy: "Just like the flower wilts, just like the grass parches." I shriveled like a quince and rotted like a fig. I will not crawl over to the tombs; I do not know what kind of people they were. None of them have my name inscribed. Did they mummify my body? Where did they stuff me? Have I become air? Maybe a simple headstone.

The bowed chrysanthemums grow closely along the nun's chambers. They are supple and velveteen. I could pluck them above my face, though they might leave yellow pollen and I am already covered in muck. I know I will not be able to witness the plethora of spring. My mother scoured the streets barefoot. Spilled milk covered her face and hair. This rock beneath my back is killing me. Maybe I should try to pass some gas. It's gone now. If I get gassy again, I will shoot straight up. I just hope that it's not a loud one in case the nun wakes up. I'll be careful. I think I will succeed.

I'm thirsty. I could soak my tongue in the rain. I could chew some drenched pine needles or stuff my mouth with mud. Thomaís, a distant cousin of mine, doesn't ring a bell. No–I wanted to say something else: Thebaids, desert, Thaís, abbess, former courtesan who tortured her filthy body on the sand and had a dry tongue. St. George the Koutalás, confessionary and psalm singer, lived out his days on a wet, shady landscape between Kesarianí and Karéa. Chakkas Marios, lyricist and victim of suicide. He frequented this spot in the morning sometimes. I brewed him coffee. What do I know.

It's raining. I know that all around me there is the mountain, from incline to incline, then the canyon. I am at the bottom. At the break of dawn, it will begin to steam. This place is nothing special, it's hidden away and ugly. I used to come on sunny days and sit on the bench next to the nun's dwelling, beside the chrysanthemum beds. She'd bring me iced water with my coffee. She owned a refrigerator. The nun is sleeping now, and when the morning comes, she'll be in for a fright. I hope nothing will happen to her when she witnesses me in this state, considering that she's a little dopey and all.

I wonder what the rest of my friends are doing—what's left of them, anyway. Tsaoúsis, who sleeps in late, might be washing his penis now, and he too will eventually join the fallen. Phaedon must have left his open palm on some woman's breast. And Fótis, if his baby is fussy, will be sleepless and broody. Oh, and Thomas is most likely hanging out at a club, unable to tell the difference between his fantasies and the clouds of smoke. Why doesn't he take some pills? It's his business. He had always wanted to fabricate his own legend, and since he would die soon, he simply set the stage. These things don't last. His job was mediocre, and he suffered through all kinds of side effects, although these were quickly overcome. The publisher sold a few of his books. He was never an optimist and on top of everything he became ill. He grew to be afraid of his own bed and everyone looked at him sympathetically; the dissolution of his social group could have contributed to this state. He was withdrawn and considered everything asinine. But these kinds of people don't just die; they attempt to hold on until the end. They have some headstone to look forward to, or they think of their families, an ideal, a purpose—they don't leave themselves high and dry. Maybe he wanted to ascribe some meaning, and therefore he offed himself in the meadow. Now, even the field lies fallow, and the nun has been taken away. She was talking to herself. They found out that the doors to the church had been left unlocked. She couldn't fathom how the doors were ajar and consequently lost her mind.

It would have been more pleasant underneath the pine tree; it's coniferous. The way it's trimmed gives it the appearance of an acacia. And still, thick drops would trickle down from it. Cypresses look like inverted umbrellas and cannot hold much water. I do not wish to touch the wall of the church—those tombs are nearby. The nun's old room is located on the other side. The only shelter is within the church. However, all the times I've visited, I've found it locked. When the nun unlatched the doors, I would pretend to make an offering by clinking something against bronze cast, as if I'd pay for the candle I would never light. The moment she'd bring my coffee and set it on the bench, she immediately locked the doors again. The keys hung from a large ring attached to her belt.

I am cold and the rain continues to shower. I don't recollect well, and I removed the stone from beneath my back; St. George, please do something about that door—come as a fierce wind and swing it open. I am aware it's not possible to enter without a set of keys and I am not expecting a miracle. What I do know for certain is that the nun was not a believer. A day before she went in for her surgery, the priest who was recovering in the bed next to her offered her a small icon, and she scornfully returned it to him. Open the door for me, I tell you, I am shivering. If you are my protector then clear the passage—I am soaked, I am numb.

The arch of the doorway somewhat protects me from the downpour. It's raining in the opposite direction so you're able to shield yourself a little bit. I hope I do not freeze before daybreak. I shook my legs and they appeared to still work. Then, I walked about and touched the church's door. It receded with a slight creak at the hinges. Most likely, since the nun was a bit slow, the door was left open again. I sauntered in. She swore she had fastened it. The key was found stuffed in a pot next to her dwelling the other day. She had said that she hid it there only on Sundays so the priest wouldn't sneak into her room during the early hours. It was the middle of the week, a Wednesday.

I lit a match, then a candle whose flame scintillated. It casted long shadows against the corners, the walls were barely lit, the candelabras danced. I glanced toward the ceiling and found it empty; there was no Creator to look at me sternly, and even if he was present, I would not care. To my left there was a brigadier general who gave the impression of cracking a slight smile. His cheek quivered a bit, and it was almost as if he was winking at me, but then again, this could have all been the flame's effect. Regardless, I winked back at him. On the right there was a man who resembled Tsaoúsis, he was sweet and defenseless, just like when Tsaoúsis served in Makronísi. I thought I saw him make a sign about some pegs, as though I would know who stole them.

They were all congregated there; the fresh asbestos bubbled and beneath it you could catch a glimpse of the old wall paintings. My friends were appearing before me—one was holding a book in his hand, the other clutched a picture of a woman I used to love, and the last bore the infamous sycamore leaf. Phaedon unfolded the parchment paper dotted with his final stanzas. The doctor wore a floor length stole that was adorned with images of women. They had normal proportions, but their faces were situated in circles. He was solemn, and his beard created a feeling of distance between himself and the world. It was like he was disappointed to offer these drawings and instead would have preferred to have stanzas on his stole.

Thomas was biting his lip again and separated himself from the others. Underneath his armpit he was holding some book, and maybe he was slipping away or losing himself in others, becoming Judas' double. I realize that I could have fabricated this after reading a forbidden gospel which conflated Thomas and Judas. Yet, he did not stand alongside the others in the group, instead he had broken off and was looking behind him while biting down on his lip.

Beside the river of Babylon, with his back to the mountains, the bouzouki player perched on his stool. On the peaks there were scores of soldiers who flooded the only ways out. In the ravines, the solitary revolutionaries of Mória were trying to conceal themselves. They were naked and starving. The bouzouki was belting out a melodic taqsim.

Neophyte walked along the coastline while holding his crippled arm. Where did you cripple it, Neophyte? I broke it while fighting for the movement, and then I was going to have an old professor of ours perform surgery on it, but he sent his assistant instead. I said forget about it, I didn't send my assistant to fight for me in the war. Now I stride over the waves to console my withered arm—and don't you think that what I said was quite clever? — his belly shook as he laughed, but again, this may have been a mirage induced by the weak candlelight.

In another corner, safeguarded from the draft, sat old Paggourélias. He was building a miniature boat—he used threads for sails, tinsel, all different types of decorations, and he placed a small flag at the top. He was steadily holding it atop his knees. Here, in this corner, the winds certainly won't blow, and the boat will never sink. He'll get out of jail at some point and marry, even though he is over seventy years old, and he'll have kids who will cradle this boat and sing carols.

And beyond the cracked plaster there was Panagákis, who looked very pleased with the new commune, and Dimítris who was grasping his paint brushes, Tímos with his untied boots and eyes swollen with sleep; they were all there supporting me. The mother with the baby in her embrace, Minister of Births, the young stud from the Ministry of Eros who was surrounded by little cherubs, and further off, the great conqueror who was gesturing to me as if to inquire about my readiness. He was holding a piece of paper and a quill to jot down everything. He covered the entire wall, the whole space. Darkness settled.

THE LAST ONES

So long as lips shall kiss
and eyes shall see
so long lives love
and love gives life to thee[8]

The bedroom appears almost nude to the walls. Only a single frame, the corner of a jail cell, and a band accompanying Genevieve's play[9]. The entire furnishing consists of two beds with their little nightstands, an old closet and the desk. As time passes, I feel as if my entire world becomes increasingly enclosed in this room. I've reached forty, and my prospects are ominous: metastatic cancer, impending consumption, the end near and unavoidable.

I know, I will never be able to get away with it. It's not that they keep telling me to stop smoking; that is just one detail of the forces that keep pushing me toward destruction. Something has always driven me toward the worst, and now that the worst has gotten out of control, it's not a matter of me becoming better, I never even wanted to be better, so let's just say that I like my

---

8. Chakkas' note: This was written underneath a poster which depicted a statue of Durga, a six-armed female goddess in Hinduism associated with strength, motherhood, war, and destruction.

9. Translator's note: This is a reference to Genevieve of Brabant.

chest to feel as if it's a boiling pot, and in my embrace I feel as if though there is a kitten that gazes at it, a companionship throughout the night that takes care of me when I wake.

My wife sleeps in the bed next to mine. I cough and cannot expel the phlegm from my lungs. It's like an engine that struggles to turn over, and just when I think that it's finally moving forward, it still labors, the sound does not stabilize, and I hear it deteriorate inside the cylinder, slowly burning out. I make other efforts, too. "What is it?" yells my wife in a drowsy state of confusion. "Nothing. Go back to bed." She shifts to her other side and continues to sleep; a little whistling sound concludes her breath.

She is a good woman. She cares for me, brings me milk in bed, and if I spill it on myself from time to time she does not complain, she fluffs my pillows, collects all of the tissues I toss onto the floor for no reason. The ten years we've been married have percolated into this calm relationship, where neither of us are disgusted by each other's spittle, and there's a distinct tenderness and understanding. Many times when she has a headache, I say to her "come," and "come here so I can caress you for a little while," and immediately her pain subsides or she calms down quite a bit. Everything is quiet and soft in this room, this is how we have settled down after ten years of living together.

But it wasn't always like this. We endured many hardships

before we reached this state. The first years of our relationship were marked by ferocity, and maybe I was to blame since from the beginning I did not make a decision to realize that I was a married man, and would always fool around, which made her wail on me. There was frustration, tears—she never let things go, so I resigned myself after a while, and then my illness became our great equalizer.

Life is one continual adjustment that leads to a bottleneck, and when you reach the end you accept this room as your assigned space, you search the ceiling and the walls in the off-chance that you'll discover some stain in the paint and you always wonder about what it looks like: a face, a thing or an animal's shape. The single frame tilts a little bit. Did I take my pill? The tissue paper is almost out. The book I am reading is banal. I need to shift sides, maybe that would ease my discomfort.

At a time I thought that if I lost my legs in a car accident I would kill myself. Now, I can't catch my breath and I am weak below the knees, so I pause every now and then and sit. I don't have legs, and yet I insist on living. I want to live the way I used to even if I don't have my strength anymore, in the streets, I don't want to change anything about my rhythm, but it, too, is idling and will stall out soon enough. I can't make it up this hill, I want to lay down, I yearn for my bed, the room with the stains, the shutters which articulate the light against the wall.

My body has betrayed me, it's as white as a bedsheet, my face like linen—a frothy storm. My body abandons me, I am left behind, I am sinking. "Don't give up," my wife hollers at me and I give it one last push.

Now, I find myself at a hotel in Paddington, at another one in Bridgewater, another in Camden; everywhere is lined with plastic carpeting, everywhere has a faucet tacked to the wall. Now, I walk along Fulham Road, I'm in Brompton, standing in front of a building with red bricks. The female doctor uses one hand to fix up some small things that look like weeds, hair, and with her other hand she holds up a plate which is projected on the x-ray screen. Her long face becomes even longer. "Unfortunately, it is what it is," she says. "I, however, am satisfied with the whole process. It's getting bigger of course, but somewhat slowly. I hope that it will not develop at a faster rate."

I exit the hospital. At the South Kensington station I see the newspapers brandishing the latest news: Lillian Board, 22 years old, European champion in the 800 meter race, dies of cancer. "She dies," write the newspapers, and for myself I think *No dice*[10], and allow the escalator to lead me into a deep descent.

Later, at the Porte d'Orléans station in Paris, I read about

---

10. Chakkas's note: No dice: something analogous to our Greek "kommeni" or "na menei".

her death. The newspapers were publicizing old photographs that depicted her at the beginning of the race, and others captured her running through the ribbon. There was one, too, in which she was walking; she had just won the 800 meter run and was smiling at the camera flashes, her face and hair like light, her chest attempting to tear through her shirt with each inhalation. I placed my finger on her chest and it immediately deflated, it was now a handful of dirt, and the photographs began to yellow, the camera flashes directed elsewhere, the record was broken yet again, the megaphones started to quiet down. We are both wedged there, at the constellation of cancer, and like this we are slowly forgotten (I saw the constellation when I was asleep one day and was startled, it was the same shape as the burden in my chest that the x-ray had illuminated). Again and again I place my fingers against the chest, I'm always searching for myself—sometimes it does not go up and down anymore, dead, and with my last effort I am barely able to cut through the ribbon.

It couldn't have happened any other way, this was its natural progression: It started the size of a chickpea, then transformed into a quarter, then an egg, and is now the size of a fist. Hope has ran out.

There are some old cafes with high ceilings and marble tables where the retirees, veterans, gather and play euchre with their donuts. Occasionally the third player is absent, possibly because of the flu or because his urea is high, so they recruit another third, and eventually devolve back to two, and one by one they disappear. They give up their seats quietly, exit the game and rest for a little bit outside of the city. This is kind of how I was hoping to fade out, and this is probably how it would have gone if this thing in my chest stopped growing.

There is a cafe in Paris, Porte d'Orléans. An old man sits in the corner and lightly rests on his cane. He is wearing army fatigues, on his head he has a patrol cap, and on one of his lapels he sports the symbol of a helm. In front of him there is a small liquor glass filled with a yellow drink. He licks it every so often. His jaw is so close to his nose that they almost mesh. The other day I went to the cafe earlier than I usually do. He was sitting there in his usual spot. The following day, I got up at the crack of dawn. He was still there. I'm now sure that he will still be there when I am unable to go anymore, and even when I can't go because I have ceased existing, even after you all, the old man will be in his seat. You can corroborate this after two or three generations—he wears a dark colored army fatigue with large lapels, on his head a blue patrol cap, and, of course, the symbol of the helm on one of the lapels. "Captain, hey, Captain, how do you manage to sail us off and remain on land? How are you able to stay while we have to depart?" He has an expressionless face, full of wrinkles, lizard's skin and a jaw that almost touches his nose. Porte d'Orléans, the corner cafe that we directly pass as we exit the metro, not the other one above, which is also situated in a corner across from the exit (the other exit). I am always talking about the one at the southern exit which is called cafe d'Orléans, or, the other one might have this name, I don't recall well, or at the corner across the street, search in need at the other corner as well, there can't be more than four of them, and mind the exits because there are many, don't become confused, don't let it slip by you, pay attention, you will miss it. I don't think you will find it in the end even though there was a good chance, it seemed so simple at the beginning but it is actually so difficult to come face to face with the old sailor.

I drag myself across the Athenian streets, I grab onto the trees and move onward. I have nothing else to grab onto anymore. Until now, many people would lean on me and I would carry them. Once, a djinn, without me realizing how and why I was related to such a thing, begged me to take him across. I hoisted him on my back and when we got there he refused to come down. For many years I walked with the jinn attached to me, and maybe this is why I am a little stooped over. I don't know how I got rid of him, I only know that the stiffness of my face is a result of the efforts to unburden myself.

Now I also need to find someone who will carry me. The bad part is that I have forsaken the time of my prime, friends and ideas included. I place some calls but most go unanswered. When I ask "are you?" to those who eventually pick up the phone, they clam up. I know that I will walk alone, but how will I survive the rest of the journey?

I meet a young girl. I take her to the hotel. Her breasts are large and they hang. I grab onto them, she starts shouting, sniveling, and always says "take me." "Where to?" I ask irascibly. "To the place where I can't take anyone." She insists on me "taking her" and offers me her breasts. I quickly put my pants on and shoot out onto the street. A burden. The question is where I will place mine.

I enter a church and hear a stern voice emerge from behind the icons: "*Οὐ περιπατήσεις ἐν τῇ σκοτία...*"[11] Scotland? I wonder. What does Scotland have to do with me walking around? "... *ἀλλ' ἕξεις ζωὴν αἰώνιον,*" The voice continues, but I don't understand how Alexis is implicated here. Life eternal yes, but where does Alexis come into play?[12] It's a cypher. It's better not to meddle with metaphysics. I search around in hopes of finding out who posited the riddle. I find an epigraph with the phrase "and I will give you rest." No, I do not need that kind of rest. I know

---

11. Translator's note: The phonetic translation of the phrase is "Ou peripatises en ti skotia..." — the word "skotia" in this sentence means darkness, but it also sounds like the Greek word for Scotland. Chakkas is making an acoustic pun on the incoherency of divine prophecy.

12. Translator's note: Similar to the preceding pun, Chakkas is playing with the words "ἀλλ' ἕξεις" (all' exeis) which sound like the Greek name Alexis.

they say the shrubbery around my body will salvage my soul. The problem for me is exactly the opposite; if it is possible for me to save the body, then I do not care at all about the soul. Send it to the cauldrons, the tar pits, let it never achieve rest, let it be an invisible little dog that makes itself known by the ringing of its bell, and let it scare the passersby who walk desolate country roads at night time so badly that they take off running. I walk backwards outside of the church.

I go to a secret meeting, post up in a corner and attempt to immerse myself in the conversations of others. For a while, I manage to lose myself in the group, but my cough emerges as to remind me of my situation, it is persistent and bothers them, I cannot assimilate with the group, I cannot become one with its goal so that when I stop existing it will continue on without me and will deliver a sense of timelessness through its members. Alchemy. Either you exist or you don't, and everything is simply a collection of consolations, that's why the goal is so large, because that way it will include many others, entire generations in fact, with one passing it on to the next, and the secret meetings become prolonged, some problems will be solved, others discovered. People forget themselves in there, they occasionally arrive at the end, they quietly think to themselves "the others will continue on," and surrender.

Half-coughing, I take the floor and just barely drop the

cue: "He who survives should save himself." Naturally, no one approves of my opinions (it's old news, and besides, no one has really listened to me anyway), so I am forced to explain to them that I will die for me and only me, I have no intentions of dying for any cause, and I will instead live it up, because this matter is solely my sentence and there's no chance I'll burden others with it. I take my leave and continue wandering.

I relax at a bar, right where the attic's stairs end. At the nearby table a girl leisurely drinks her coffee. The waitress comes up the stairs with a full tray in hand. Hunched over, I speak to the girl confidentially:

"Would you like me to cause the waitress to fall?" and just before I can smooth out the conversation I hear the crash of glasses behind me. I run toward the waitress.

"My apologies," I tell her.

"How come you're apologizing?" she asks while dusting herself off. "How is this your fault, Sir?"

Of course I cannot explain any of this to her and return to my seat. I feel quite powerful after this event, my cough has disappeared, my legs touch down firmly on the attic floor. The girl stares at me intently as if to say "that wasn't right," she's left her coffee half-finished, she neurotically crosses her legs, flings a deluge of hair off of her shoulders. I want to continue playing my role, but I don't want her to think that I'm a clown.

"I am gifting you a tuft of my hair," I say and rip out as much hair as my palm fits (it's falling out due to the medication anyway, and every time I tug on it strands linger on my hands). As time passes, her charm seduces me even more. I am ready to offer her my one eye (and it isn't even glass), but I unfortunately don't have a fork to gouge it out—I want to give her whatever I have with me and even double that, obviously not the kidney though, because I've already removed one, but generally speaking whatever she asks of me is hers. It seems that the attraction is mutual, I am also bewitching her in some way because I don't want her to believe that I'm a clown, or to have an untrue opinion about me. Whatever I do, I do according to the rules of objective reality, I am not deceitful; if anything I am simply a strange man.

"Are you coming?" I ask without revealing if I want her to come to my table or the nearest hotel or that grand trip. She nears close. She's tall, her legs statuesque and endless. I've always desired a tall woman. All the ones that crossed my path were stubby, and they sprained their necks trying to look at me. I abandon my pitiful posture, sit proudly, and I finally smile (I do so for my situation and how it's looking brighter), I feel a force flood my hands. I lift my fist and land it on the machine—those ones that measure how strong you are. Inside, the puck rises, and everyone expects it to stop at sixty, or at most seventy. The puck lunges, suprasses onehundred and catapults out. Many look at me with awe, others take notice of my weak limbs and remain in disbelief. "For you, my love," I whisper and discreetly distance myself from the crowd. She encourages me by smiling. Now, the supernatural force has reached my legs. I go up the mountain almost running, I reach the peak first, I light my cigarette and wait for the others. "For you, my love," I repeat, and she in turn hugs and kisses me.

"I can achieve many things," I tell her.

"Don't worry, you'll get well," she responds.

"But you won't leave, regardless of whether or not I become well."

"No, no," she assures me. "I will forever stay by your side."

"If you don't I'll slash you, I'll make you ugly by cutting two lines into your cheek. I will write my initials on your flesh, an X, so that you will always be mine."

"I'll pack on a thick layer of makeup and it won't be apparent."

Then I begin to search for her all across her face, "it's not you," I dig my nails deep into her skin, "it's not you," I scrape the paint and finally uncover the etchings: "It's you. Are you coming?"

"Where?"

"Everywhere, even in the deepest darkness. I, however, will walk in the dark some day."

"Yeah, yeah, in Scotland. There is a specialized research center for your illness. They are testing out new methods. You'll see, you'll get better. They spike your fever to forty-one and a half by dumping oxygen and helium in the lungs."

"To Scotland then?" I say wondering. "And Alexis, how do you explain Alexis? Not that it really interests me to have "eternal life," but I ask out of curiosity."

"A lexeis, where the article a is referent and the verb is in the future tense of speaking and asking—as in what you will say in the future—these are the only things that can reach eternity."

"So words and loving," I continued mumbling.

"You need to write, and maybe your writing will survive you."

This is how this fight about words continued on, and the other fight too, the one with women; these are the two things that expelled me beyond the world's borders, they hurled me into the chaoses and I said that I would never return from there, until the point I return to reality for a little bit, where I concern myself with my illness before departing again.

"I took him so that I can lift him up high," said the other woman.

"And then he will fall and wipe out," my wife responded.

"It has to do with a therapeutic method," I interjected. I was laying down in bed and the pillows were propping my head up high. I breathed with difficulty.

"We need to boost his morale," said the other woman again.

"Without anything in sight? Where will he lean on?" my wife insisted.

"We will pursue an increase in temperature," I put myself in the middle again in an attempt to reconcile the two. They were standing to the right and the left of the bed and their eyes lit up like lightning. "I am going to reach forty, maybe forty-one, the badness will burn up inside of me and then I will slowly come back down to my normal limits."

"What I know," my wife said with bitterness in her voice, "is that you need to have steady footing, delusions are not allowed anymore."

"His elevation is necessary, or else he will sink, he'll turn inwards and he will never come out again."

"I'll keep him where he is," she responded stubbornly and made a gesture to grab onto the bed.

"When I come back down I will pass by here again, don't worry, and you can both assist me by retaining me at thirty-six and six, that way I won't go too further down, so the treatment will work, but the patient…"

"It is not certain that you will pass by here again when you come down. Your space is vast, and your abilities are limitless. The problem you face is beginning, you won't be buried in this room," said the tall woman and gave the bed a strong push. My wife tried to hold on to it, but I stood up on my own, barely having any time to grab a sheet because I wasn't wearing anything. I reached the ceiling feeling light. Down below they were fighting, they'd even put their hands on each other.

"Leave," yelled the tall one, and my wife responded with "stay." I almost yielded. I saw the little frame on the wall tilt and thought to myself that I should come down to straighten it. Next, I caught the tall one's gaze, it was austere, as if she realized what was going on and was able to win me over again.

"From where?" I yelled to her, while at the same time the sheet slipped and was about to reveal something.

She rushed toward the window and my wife scurried behind her. She quickly opened one of the panes.

"I can't fit through there," I exclaimed.

My wife fastened the other pane. "Let's see who the stronger one is," I thought, and the tall one violently pushed her and they both fell onto the bed while fighting.

"Leave," shouted the tall one while struggling, and I insisted on seeing whether or not my wife still wanted me, if she would cry out "stay," but the other one had put her hand over her mouth and only a grunt slipped out. I performed a little volplane and upon opening the other windowpane, I heard my wife's desperate voice "don't, she is going to destroy you."

"It's in my best interest" I retorted and couldn't bear to stick around to give her any more explanations—the oxygen and helium had inflated my lungs and I was gaining elevation.

On the first floor my brother-in-law was fixated on re-upholstering a tattered chair.

"Where are you going?" he asked me while bent over.

"Greetings to the bridesmaid," I responded and happily waved my hand.

"Where to?"

"Up there. It's a new therapeutic method, something like space travel."

He wished me "good luck" and continued working on his chair. In the loft my other brother-in-law was reading some book. His hair was a bird's nest and his eyes red, possibly from staying up all night.

"I'd either go up or down, but I couldn't stay where I was any longer," I tried explaining myself to him.

"I am sorry. I am sorry," he responded quickly because he wanted to rid himself of me and get back to his book.

"Please tell the women down there to stop arguing, because I am long gone now, and even if I wanted to I can't stick around," I said and adjusted the sheet over myself, bringing one corner over my shoulder and letting the rest of it hang down to my feet.

"I don't get involved in other people's family problems. But, I still wish you a good trip. If you don't come back, can I make use of your library for some of my studies?"

"Of course, I allow you to work on my literary project," I shouted back at him and left.

I was sinking in a deep, milky substance and was constantly losing myself. The tall one and my wife had gone out to the yard and were looking up at me using some smoked lenses, but I disappeared into a cloud and could not distinguish anything, and I believe they could not see me either. A certain loneliness enveloped me, I was a little cold, why didn't I grab a blanket as I was leaving, my teeth were chattering, why did I only bring the sheet, I suppose I wanted to present myself as a Jesus figure and now I was shivering, I gathered myself up like a ball of yarn, and just as the air thinned out, I made more of an effort to breathe. My body was flaming inside, the oxygen combined with the helium were burning up my entrails, they were opening up bronchi dammed by smoking many years ago. The fever was increasing in waves, going from violet to red and from light blue to dark, and after that gray arrived, and beyond that I saw a variant of black approaching me—it was a giant centipede—"it reached forty already,"[13] I thought to myself. It covered me, walked all over me and tickled my body. I was shaking, hopping up and down, "What

13. Translator's note: In Greek, centipedes are called "forty-legs."

is that thing that will make me reach forty-one, what is that worse thing?"

I had already gone through the six colors and only the seventh remained, my blood boiled, my heart thumped like an out of control jazz drum, and when the blackest black slithered the way that an octopus does, it seized me, I was lost, at any moment I'd find myself at the limits, but I would be alright as long as I did not surpass them and was able to observe things from the other side. I was on the verge, my forehead was a hot spring spurting out water, my hair was melting, I looked into the asphalt"s blackness and yelled with all of the strength that I had left "Euridice, Euridice," no answer, not even my voice's echo returned, it was lost in the chaos, "Euridicc," I insisted, but I couldn't even hear my own voice anymore.

I was still holding on to the verge, but I felt forces push me in, I barely held on and kept my legs out with difficulty, the other half of my body had already passed through, "forty and a half," I heard someone say nearby me. When I whispered "Lillian Board," I heard my voice multiply over dozens of speakers and become tangled with the crowd's cries. "Lillian Board," I said more steadily and saw her run toward me like a light in the dark. It was her, leaping like a doe, holding a torch—she was at a distance of about four hundred meters and was coming directly to me. I began feeling heavy, my trajectory turned downward, I threw my arms back and fell ever so slowly in the direction that Lillian's light carved out. The darkness was slipping away. "Thirty-nine and a half," I heard and everything around me was stained violet. "I will take her home, too," I thought, and looked back to see if she was coming. Now she was running in the opposite direction, she was becoming smaller, so small that she transformed into a little dot, and at the end she froze in place and became a tiny star.

I continued my descent, and everything around me was whitish, clouds, maybe even sheets, I thought. At a distance, the houses looked frightened; they brushed up against each other and kept warm. Then I discerned trees, naked acacias, and I said to myself "deep Fall," and as I made my way there, I clearly saw the stone fence and despite my effort to land outside of it, I eventually landed on the inside. I fell straight into a ditch surrounded by people, some of which were tossing in flowers—they covered my face, someone threw a handful of dirt, it was soiling my clothes and I thought I should dust it off of me, but I could not distinguish between my hands and the dirt, as they were both the same color and meaty, and anyway the dirt matched my clothes. Another man tossed a wad of pebbles up high, it seemed that the dirt ran out, and immediately after him the other guy threw a large rock which landed on my knee and knocked me out. There were quite a few of my acquaintances, and right in front stood my wife wearing a weeping veil, further behind her stood the tall one wearing a tight dress, and she turned me on a little bit as she tried to make room in the crowd to reach me because she was doing strange dancing movements which showed off her breasts, her high cheekbones, her legs, ah. My God, her endless legs, her hands were talking as she approached me and then she leaned on me, she dragged me out from underneath a rain of rocks, I latched on to her, I stalled and sought her lips.

"It's not the right time for these kinds of things," she said sternly. "Toss in a handful of dirt or something so that we can cover him."

The rest were now shoveling, some pushed dirt into the grave with their feet because they did not want to get dirty, three people worked together to carry an enormous stone, and someone threw a trash can filled to the brim. So, I symbolically cast a pebble in there and parted with the girl. I exited the fence and the tall one linked arms with me in a protective way, as if she was consoling me, as if she was standing by me, and I immediately took advantage of the situation by recommending a hotel.

"I have time," I told her. "Now that everyone thinks that I am buried in there," and started to look for a taxi, "we will lock ourselves in a room and no one will bother us." Once again I was impatient, and because no taxi was in sight I had to adjust my proposition: "Look, we can go here, behind the little pine trees, we can have a quickie," and I was already unbuttoning myself, I couldn't hold out anymore.

"You can't waste your strength on such things," she said once again in her stern way.

"But it is not a waste. This is how I am reborn."

"You should pour all of your strength into your writing."

"Words and loving," I reminded her.

"First come the words and then the loving."

They told me that they will make me well, in a way of speaking, that I will be able to breathe, move my arms, and every now and then I will go on a walk, as long as I don't waste away of course, especially as it concerns my writing.

In my response to them I asked if there was a possibility for me to write even if it meant that I couldn't walk, that I couldn't move my arms at all, that I couldn't even breathe. They lifted their hands up high pointing toward an abstract direction. I went there.

There was one guy with a big white beard, he was holding a long string of worry beads which he slowly thumbed through. I explained to him that there was no way, I don't want any favors, but because I started writing at an older age, thirty years old and then some, and because, as it seems, I cannot go beyond forty, and in other words since I am running out time and still have a few images in my mind, I think that they shouldn't go to waste. They're these weird thoughts that maybe no one else will have after me, just one more book, not too big, just a little thicker than the last one, two or three fingers in width. And primarily, the book will not be written against anyone. Against myself perhaps, against my nose that is kind of big and is more pronounced when I lose weight, my eyebrows which lighten and are suspect, my beady eyes. And yet the girls still ran after me.

The guy with the white beard looked at me fixedly. He was not glum, nor was he pompous. He was unrelenting though, and in his gaze there was the abyss.

"You are an egoist as well," he says. "You don't approach me in order to beg me to grant you more years of life, but you ask me the impossible, to transgress my principles: To keep writing even when your Bic pen has ran out. No, this cannot happen. Every day the sun will rise."

"Listen," I retorted, "don't get on my nerves, because I am going to buckle down and write it in two or three months, I will write it on my knees if push comes to shove (and the way you're directing things, secondly, there won't be any time left for neat handwriting, and thirdly if there is a possibility for a tenth draft, editing, all of these things are only superfluous details, since you are pressing me for time). In any case I will surely write it and it will be against you, a provocation, it will be about how I went up to her and brought her near to the bed, how we both fell onto one another like rabid dogs, how the garter belts were tricky. Don't play with your worry beads neurotically, these are things that you have never done and you can't even imagine what happened on the bed that night."

His face was marbled, an "unbreakable wall,"[14] and I searched for a crack, a little tremor so that I can slide through it and make it out alive on the other side, just to write this book, not forever, we are not even talking about the average life span here, maybe just about the next five years which could have been my most fertile, a small exception, a medicine that will keep the tumor at the same spot for four or five years, not a cure, the danger of looming consumption, the way that I will always be looking at his marbled face in search of a fissure, and as I can't find it, I will become increasingly miniscule as I sweat, up until the final rattle is recorded.

A time will come when I will drop to my knees and plead for one more day. Once I hear the people around me whisper "this is the eschaton," while they lift their hands up high toward an abstract direction, then I will again beg for at least one

14. Translator's note: Chakkas is drawing from an Orthodox hymn which is dedicated to the Virgin Mary.

more day, and if he is merciful, he will grant it to me even though I have dragged him through so much in the meantime.

On the right-hand side there'll be my wife, on the left the tall one, and they will both wash my feet with an exorbitantly expensive cologne. A waste, some might think, of this just to show that there were people who did not approve of me even until the very end. And actually this cologne is necessary, because I have many different scents on me, vomit, urine due to incontinence, sour sweat, and the cologne conceals all of these, in a way that even the girls in the band and Genevieve don't turn their faces, on the contrary, they too shower the corpse in their own way.

At the head of the bed my mother tears out her hair, sobs intensely, so much so that I cannot bear to listen to her. "More quietly," I gesture to her and she grabs a sliding book of funerary lamentations.[15]

These are the women who encircle me first, they stand by me irreconcilably, though, due to the fact that my wife took my mother's son, and my girlfriend took my wife's husband. Tomorrow someone else will take me, and this way they will be able to reconcile. In the end I always find somewhere to belong, I never belonged to myself. "Don't argue," I whisper, "they only gave me one more day, and this was a result of my begging, I clench

---

15. Translator's note: This is a reference to Greek funerary practices. The mourners share a book of lamentations and read them out loud.

my teeth to try and hold on to it, it is not completely a freebie, I need to divulge some kind of effort."

Thankfully, I divided my body correctly, and they each received an arm and a leg, but my genitals were excluded because the cologne stings them, the belly button and my sternum's ribs are separated by a straight line, the neck, the adam's apple, the jaw, the peak of my nose a landmark, the figurative line passes between my eyebrows and divides my forehead. I keep my hair in case one of them wants to brush it one way and the other another way, I don't want to present a ridiculous scene. Of course, my wife is allocated the surgical scar, loses the heart, but this is how it must be, it's always on the right side and I shouldn't misunderstand it. I turn and look at Genevieve and the band. She is always ready to ride a horse and depart. "Hold on," I tell her soullessly, "tomorrow we'll leave together." She looks like the girl I used to love when I was fourteen years old; she also let her blonde hair loose and her skin was the same rosy tint. The Easter lamb grazed in the forest, and when the time came to slaughter it, she sobbed so desperately that they let it go. I was attending middle school then and used to read in the forest (there was no room at home, we only had one bedroom and a kitchen for four people—the Kesarianí mahallah) but God still loved me, because the lamb would follow me from behind and would bring the girl near me. It was still pleasant that spring under the pines, our footsteps moved in tandem with the lamb's bell, we rolled in the grass, little Genevieve, the lamb and myself, the book tossed way out there and the sun smiling between the pine needles. From time to time God revealed a small part of his white beard—the tattered remains of a pillowy cloud in the sky which then disappeared again and left the forest cloudless. Until one day, I suddenly heard my mother's voice from behind me: "Hey you, is this your homework?" She had her hands hoisted on her waist, and flames and smoke rose from her nostrils, just like the beast from the book of Revelations. The lamb ran off scared, and the girl readjusted herself in a way where I saw her white underwear and how, out of fear, she had peed a little bit. "And you, you minx," my mother tells her, "why are you seducing him? I am going to tell your mother everything." When I went back to the forest the next day, the lamb had been slaughtered and the girl's hair was tightly braided. My mother was obviously satisfied with this because she had brought me back onto God's path, that's how she used to say, even though I never again saw God's face, it was like he was preying on me, and he constantly revealed himself as far as it concerned girls, and later when I snagged a chick who allowed me to grab her breasts, they grew and became like stone, I didn't squeeze them, I simply caressed them lightly and ran my hand over them wondering why I could not find a nipple that looked like the ones I had seen when the new mothers fed their babies, big and red like a ball, and he caught me in the act again with my hand on her bust when it got tangled in her strangely constructed bra, that wretched thing, my hand could not come out.

Now she is sniveling at the head of the bed, and if I remind her of these old circumstances, she might tell me that I am in this position precisely because of those sins and that I must at least repent at the last moment. The other day she got a candle that was as large as myself, and bought a little human made of silver, and ran to Jesus of Spáta in case she could save me. I now know that she will insist on me partaking in Holy Communion. I do not oppose it. Toward the end, though, toward my expiration, I will pretend to open my mouth, and I will snatch the communion chalice from the priest and I will begin blessing him, my mother, my wife, and my side chick. Why? Just because, that's why. When I asked for the Lord's protection, he told me "I can't give it to you." Why should I die at forty, while others reach seventy and eighty? And myself aside, let's say forty is enough, why did Lillian die at twenty-two? Was it because she didn't exercise? Did she have a bad diet or did she smoke? Who is the one who gives and takes and dies on Saturday? Justice.

I don't want mercy, I don't want mercy, my God (this proclamation, My God, is a sigh which stems from the plumage of my heart and not an invocation).
Because I do not have wrongs for you to eradicate
iniquities for you to wash away
and sins for you to cleanse.
I would be the first one to recognize my transgressions and my sins
as they would forever condemn me in my own eyes.
No one, no one has been subject to my harm and I have not done anything wicked on behalf of another, so I cannot justify your words and accept your judgment.
I will not accept that my parents are at fault and that my mother was impregnated with me by sin.
I search but cannot find the truth, the secret and unrevealed have always remained
unknown to me.
Bless me with the seeds of oregano and myrtle, thyme's dust, the mountain's
moss and maybe this way I will be cleansed and become whiter than snow.
I hear music and rejoice, my tired little bones
jubilate.
Look, look at how my pure heart is reflected on my face and how from deep within me
my earnest soul rises.
Do not turn your face into an obstacle, allow me to see it and
beyond it.

GUILTY OF GUILT

It's as if they slid me through a mail slot into a downward sloping room. The area was nightmarish and the descent so slippery that I didn't expect it when I began—it continued beneath my feet and I couldn't discern the end.

I felt a small assurance when I sat on a bench, though I realized that I was only temporary, they couldn't just leave me forever with my legs hanging, and I predicted that I would slide further down, continuing this slippery route.

To my right, with her face toward me, sat a woman at a small old desk. She was fifty, maybe sixty, dry, she wore little glasses with round lenses and a wire frame, possibly tall, and she had a black jacket thrown over her back. I would call her a pawn shop employee or a hospital secretary who had aged doing this job, this is how she presented herself based on her movements and the comfortable way that she checked the various things that were stacked on the small desk.

"May I help you?" she said, and instead of giving her an answer I smiled.

"What do you want?" her voice was harsher this time.

"Nothing," I told her and continued to smile idiotically.

"I hope they didn't bring you by force?" she asked and gestured in a way that seemed like she was trying to shoo me, but maybe it was a tic or perhaps she was shooing away a fly at that moment, I don't know.

"No," I rushed to answer, "they didn't force me to come. The truth is that I didn't understand how I got here. Maybe I was doing something like playing, I was searching at the shore, then I thought to myself that I might find something else further down, and I was slipping all the time."

"Of your own volition, then," said the woman and signed something on a piece of paper.

"There's the slipping also," I dared to say once I saw how my answers were being logged.

"Excuses. You were searching at the shore, weren't you? You could have been at the levee. Didn't you descend further down of your own volition? Of course, the unstable ground contributed to your descent, too. All of these things will be written down, don't worry."

"I always take account of my responsibilities," I said and pretended that I was going to step my foot down, but the woman prevented me from doing so with her pointed finger, I even caught a small chuckle, this is what I surmised based on the wrinkles around her mouth, and I thought for a moment that maybe things will change for the better, but I immediately regretted it, her gaze was unsparing, it was turned to me in a penetrating and persistent way which made my stomach turn and I had the impression that if someone supported me, it would bring me relief. I wanted a person like a twin brother next to me, like a classmate who had worse grades than me, a colleague who shared the blame with me at some job so that when we got called in to fess up he would take on half of the blame and even more, a co-defendant with graver charges, maybe he could be the main defendant.

THE WOMAN (abruptly): You were born?

X. (absentmindedly): Alone. (Maybe this was a conclusion drawn from my previous thoughts.)

THE WOMAN: Unfortunately, this is the most common case. (She said it like it was a consolation for me—her mood had changed again—like a consolation for herself.)

X. : I would like for things to be different.

THE WOMAN : They don't ask us.

X. : It wouldn't be a bad thing.

THE WOMAN : Did you know that some people kill their own mothers in order to be born? Is this perhaps how you also began?

X. : No, I don't have such a thing against me.

THE WOMAN : They give their life to bring you to the light and you constantly seek the darkness. You don't stand at the clearing, at the plateau they bequeath you, you instead wedge yourselves in crevices and go looking. Looking for what?

X. : Looking out of curiosity for something different.

THE WOMAN : And what did you find?

X. : Nothing.

THE WOMAN : You drove your life into a ditch and didn't find anything in the end.

X. : Maybe I could find something. It appears that I had an ugly beginning, I accumulated weight from the start, I never felt care-free, just one difficult breath, surrounded by insecurity.

THE WOMAN : When did you begin?

X. : The year of the big crisis.

THE WOMAN : Month?

X. : A wintry one, the moon was in cancer.

THE WOMAN : Day?

X. : A cold one, with light rain, the place was dirtied by the snow that melted.

THE WOMAN : Daytime or nighttime?

X. : Close to daybreak. Dawn was approaching or maybe it was already there. Somewhere between day and night.

THE WOMAN : I'll write down thirty past four so we can be proper.

X. : I don't care. You can leave it blank.

THE WOMAN : That's not possible. You were born at a particular moment and that needs to be noted, we can't omit it. Nothing remains blank on these documents, even the time of death needs to be completed.

X. : But you can't know that.

THE WOMAN : We know plenty enough.

X. : In other words, in other words, please explain this particular circumstance.

THE WOMAN : This matter does not concern me.

I turned to look upward. The crack appeared like a beam of light, but it was a lot further away from what I initially calculated. I tried to look downward. There was no central light on the ceiling, I don't know if there even was a ceiling. Only the desk light, which was directed to me, illuminated the sloping room, and that up to a point, because there was old furniture stacked toward the bottom, dressers, closets, little metal beds, and all of these blocked up the wall, if of course there was a wall behind these things and they weren't positioned in such a way that hid the big incline.

"Will you declare anything?" asked the woman with a typical tone, and I had the sense that whatever I'd declare depended on my luck, and I immediately felt like I had come down only to declare the things that the woman asked of me.

I took my watch off. I don't remember how it reached the woman's hands on the other side. She put on a black loupe and looked at it as if she was examining it, but only from the outside and without opening the lid to see the inner mechanism. I was frightened for a moment because it was dead, it showed "thirty past four," but she dryly said "one dollar" and tossed my watch in a drawer. She then took my wedding ring and placed it on a scale, just like the ones the sarafs have. "One dollar," she said again, and I gave my wallet right after that, my cufflinks, a keychain with three keys, a clutch screw pencil that my godfather had given me when I was little and hadn't worked since that time, and the woman evaluated the worth of these things as one dollar with the same professional and indifferent voice. I suddenly found a few mothballs in my suitjacket's pocket. "Autumn," I thought and a little nostalgia almost won me over, it even seemed to me that I could smell the dirt, and something like a fainting spell was creeping up when the woman brought me back to reality:

"Will you give me the pocketknife?" and although it didn't come off like she was pressuring me, I surrendered the pocketknife because I wanted to show good conduct and because I didn't really need it. Next, I unglued my gold tooth, even though she did not ask for it, but I was sure that it might have looked like I let out a placatory laugh just a moment ago and I didn't want her to find an opportunity to tell me off later.

"Can I smoke?" I asked her.

"Of course. But you must be economical, because your share does not exceed ten dollars," she said advisingly, "and you don't know how long you will stay."

"Who knows how long I will stay?" I quickly lit the cigarette.

"In any case, it does not depend on me," said the woman indifferently. "If you wish to know, it depends much more on you yourself."

"Like what, exactly, could I do?"

"You can change your category. Now you are in the "C" category, the worst one."

"Which one should I go to? Up or down? Should I become "B" or "D"?"

"It's all very complicated and I can't explain it to you precisely. In any case, the linearity of the alphabet does not matter at all. Category "G" is worse than "J," but it is much better than "Q." In the end, what is important for you is to change, if of course there are still the margins to do so, because you made many mistakes, you must admit it, you almost reached the crime and I will not hide from you the fact that your case is one of the worst ones. Plenty of opportunities were still given to you to improve your position, but you slipped further down to the worst. Not once did you make a move toward the better, it's amazing, not once."

I started to complain and she cut me off abruptly:

"Don't deny it, it is all written down. Maybe there are a couple of exaggerations, but in general it is all correct.," and she abstractly showed the folder. "Anyway, you will be given the opportunity to rectify them, if you are able to, that is."

I did not speak. Who knows how many others had crossed through here and had testified for me. Maybe they knew everything, and maybe other things which I ignored, lies and mischief which are not missed in this world. That folder really did contain a lot of things, and they must have known much more than myself.

The woman started to make a phone call. It was an old device that had no numbers on the display, and it had a small crank handle which she turned every so often and yelled "give me a line," and would wait for a little afterward and then again turned the crank handle while yelling even more.

"They didn't see you come in?" she asked for a moment. "No way," she said and again continued with the phone. "They must be lazing about," she mumbled. She stood up and yelled with all of her strength into this siphon that looked just like the ones that ships have, but much smaller, they are on the deck, maybe they are vents or maybe megaphones for emergencies. No answer. She neurotically tried the crank handle again, and then turned to me: "Is it possible they didn't see you?"

"What do I care," I said once I saw that she had lost her cool and didn't control the situation anymore or that they weren't giving her any attention.

"It should concern you very much. I do not like this delay at all. Something serious must be happening with you. I should have understood this of course, it's not random, category "C" and you can smoke as many cigarettes as you want, no economizing necessary."

Again I looked upward and was frightened. It was completely smooth and almost vertical. I wondered how I came down from that place. Toward the bottom it was slightly more level. Now I could see better. Where you could find the woman's desk was leveled land, and at another two or three points there were plateaus forming of similar shape. The closest one to me, though, was the woman's.

Suddenly, from behind one of the closets emerged a small human of advanced age, wearing a coat and a slightly loose black tie. In his hand he was holding a folder which he placed on a table on the central plateau.

"Why are you yelling?" asked the woman sternly. "We saw him, but we first had to find the classified file. Any moment now the supervisor will arrive."

He went to the plateau on the left-hand side and started

testing out the lights while he stood there. He must have been something like a clerk, at a lower level than the woman, but he might also have secretly played a more important role, he might have had a mysterious ability which the woman suspected or which he insinuated though the way he carried himself, without mentioning it obviously, maybe it was even forbidden for him to do so, but it was in his best interest to spread himself around because of the benefits.

"That sweater suits you very much. I saw one of the same color in the storage room."

"It's the same one. They gave it to me from the lost and found. It's a little big, that's why I toss it over my shoulders."

"You even find beautiful things," said the short guy and loosened his tie a bit more. "This tie is from the storage room too, it's silk, and the knot comes undone. But I don't always catch it in time," and he glanced meaningfully toward the woman. "Others get the better things."

He did not receive an answer. The short guy continued talking and his voice had a whistle at the end of the phrase:

"The bigwigs take the best things, they take them for their wives, even their girlfriends."

Again he did not receive an answer from the woman, it was obvious that she was afraid of him, she did not want to expose herself, because who knows in which direction the short guy would take things. She only said:

"What will happen with him?" and her voice had a certain toughness.

"If the supervisor does not come, nothing will happen," and he went to the central plateau to fix the lights. "Sharp objects, pocket knife, nail clipper, razor, all okay?" he asked the woman as he adjusted the projector.

"He gave them up on his own."

"He wasn't searched?"

"He came out of his will. I have orders from the supervisor to not search people who come out of their own will."

"Yes," said the short guy, "but I am the one who approaches them. I do not like these liberals. The more calm he seems, the more dangerous he may be," he said while hunched over and picking at the cables, which is why his voice sounded asthmatic, he was struggling a little bit too, and there was also that familiar whistle at the end of his sentences. "Remember the old man from the other day, and how when I approached him, he pinched me. My leg still hurts."

In that moment the lights turned on at the central plateau and at the same time a tall, muscular man came in. He was wearing a new suit and was holding papers in his hands, too. His cheeks and shoes were shining. "The supervisor," I thought to myself and I was not wrong, it was apparent from the way that the woman stood up, and how the short guy who was already standing fixed his loose tie. The supervisor sat in an armchair at the central plateau and crossed his legs. To his left there was the short guy, and to his right was the woman who took some documents out of her desk drawer.

SUPERVISOR : Can we begin?
SHORT GUY : Everything to perfection.
THE WOMAN : He matches the documents completely.
SHORT GUY : A search was not carried out because he came on his own.
SUPERVISOR : Did you come of your own volition?
X. : Not completely. They helped me quite a bit, at least they pushed me at the beginning, they gave me my initial speed, I was sliding and couldn't not move forward. Let's say because of an accrued velocity.
SUPERVISOR : In any case, you accepted your arrival, there were some moments in which you said "how nice it is that I was born."
X. : There were also other moments when I resentfully asked "why was I born."
SUPERVISOR : So why, then, did you not put an end to it?
SHORT GUY : Did he commit suicide? He didn't. So…
X. : I thought that things might get better as they progressed.

SUPERVISOR : So, you were hoping. This is the admission. Do you agree?
X. : Under the condition that I was not asked from the beginning about this circumstance, and that others made decisions if decisions were made, and that I admit to it as a final fact that emerged ex post facto.
SUPERVISOR : So be it. Ex post facto. (To the woman) Write: Ex post facto. (To X.) And now I have another question: You were baptized, weren't you?
X. : It is the same circumstance. They baptized me.
SUPERVISOR : It is not actually the same circumstance, at least not the same for you, because aside from the name that they gave you, you acquired a second one on your own, a certain pseudonym, and this means that you liked it quite a bit. Generally, it seems that you were supportive of names, since you also baptized a child some time ago, and you even gave it a ridiculous name.
X. : It was my grandmother's.
SUPERVISOR : You could have quit, you could have put your foot down at the last moment and refuse to burden the child with that ridiculous name. You messed the child up for the rest of its life with the name Pagona. Why didn't you give it a lighthearted name, why didn't you name it Myrto, Chloe, or Aura?
X. : I would have named it something like that if it weren't for grandma.

SUPERVISOR : Of course, we could say that you were respecting family traditions. Conservative, clearly, but we can log it in your virtues.

THE WOMAN : Certainly.

SUPERVISOR : But you were in support of naming, right?

X. : Does it have a special significance?

SUPERVISOR : It does and more. You have made fun of names all of your life, you twisted words, you altered meanings. Why do you use the name Bitzídou?[16] What do you think is funny about the name Oulkérogloúmou, and is that last "mou" a part of the name or is it the possessive pronoun? Who is this man Oulkérogloúmou and this woman Bitzídou anyway?

X. : He is my customer.

SUPERVISOR : And Bitzídou?

X. : Also my customer.

SUPERVISOR : And the "mou"?

X. : Well, he is my customer.

SUPERVISOR : Is that how you write his name on his label? Why do you use "mou" only for him?

X. : Alright. He is more sympathetic to me because he is about to go bankrupt.

---

16. Translator's note: Chakkas is making another acoustic pun—the name Bitzídou sounds similar to the word used for busty women.

SUPERVISOR : And Bitzídou, is she a Miss or a Missus?
X. : Missus, but I call her Miss, she is an older girl and I don't want to offend her.
SUPERVISOR : What is your relation to Bitzídou?
X. : None. She is just Oulkérogloúmou's most stable customer, maybe the only one, and she buys various useless things in case she can support him, even though she knows well that he gets further in the hole with each passing day, there is no escape for him, but she persists so much that it moves me, and when I say her name many people think that I am using it only because of its silly sound.
SUPERVISOR : This is true. Everything else is fabricated, you concoct a story just so that you can justify your actions to us and to yourself. Why do you call Hesperus Anesperus, using a privative to immediately strip him of meaning?[17] Why do you continuously play with words as if they are devoid of meaning? You mock them, you make them differential, you say "bitch" and we are not sure if that word means bed or something else. Look, you are not walking on the right path, not the right path at all, you even slip on words. Stop jeering. The words will turn against you. "Stop jeering," interjected the short guy. "We don't tolerate fool-

17. Translator's note: In Greek, when the prefix "a" is added to a word, it strips the word of its original meaning. This grammatical addition is called "a privative." Chakkas is, in a sense, castrating Hesperus.

ishness here."

"Certainly," said the supervisor. "We take our job seriously here. When we say dog we mean dog and nothing else. Really, did this case with the dogs occur before you went to school or after?"

"I don't understand what you mean," I answered. And I truly did not remember any case about dogs.

The supervisor motioned at the woman, and she started looking through the folder. Eventually, she pulled out a paper.

"There is a testimony," said the woman, "that you called some kid dogface. You called him that first and it stuck to him. This nickname tormented him all of his life."

"Did you love dogs?" asked the supervisor.

"I don't think so."

"There's the thread," and he looked at the short guy knowingly. The short guy got up from his chair very slowly and took a thick ruler into his hands and started to twirl it. He suddenly slammed it forcefully on the desk, the dust flew into the air.

"You must remember that it is related to dogs," said the supervisor.

"From what I remember, I used to stone them when they were stuck. Later I'd stone them when they were alone, when I would find them isolated, out of habit."

"This is it," said the supervisor and stood up. "Continue."

"Naturally, I chased a handful of neighborhood strays," I continued. "I didn't dare throw rocks at fenced dogs. The moment I saw a big dog I yelled "mama" and ran so that I could hide near her. She would then turn back to her conversation and say: "You just can't imagine how scared of dogs this child is."

"Good job," the supervisor interrupted, "say it all, anything you remember."

"I later threw a rock at a kid from another neighborhood, and that must be who you mentioned, because I now remember that he had a face like a dog's. It must have been him, because once he saw me would start sprinting just like a dog and he'd disappear around the corner. Occasionally he would come by with his father, maybe they were going shopping, so I of course could not throw a rock. I would then follow him from a distance and would make some motions that only he could see, I pretended to yell "dogface, dogface" irrelevantly in the other direction. I don't have another case to mention, and if this is the one you were implying, then this is how things generally went and I take responsibility."

"No one talked about responsibilities," said the supervisor.

"These are minor offenses," said the short guy by inserting himself in the middle; he had again placed the ruler on the desk.

"Of course, of course, these events don't count in the grand scheme of things," completed the supervisor. "They are brought up as insignificant details. In these cases, we are more so interested in motive, the methods and the overall operation. Just like the cat. We want to know where this case with the cat started from, because it is a little strange."

"The motives?" I asked.

"Yes, the motives, and the deeper ones at that."

"I was opening the door very slowly. Next to me stood my little sibling, must have been two, and he suddenly screeched but I didn't understand why, and I continued opening the door, and he screamed even more, until I realized that that he had wedged his finger in the door hinge and I was slowly but surely squeezing it further. I should have understood it when I heard the first yell, I should have understood it, and the finger had a deep cut, I kissed his finger and a cold sweat took over me, I caressed it and the child kept crying. Since then I frequently hear the screeching and crying in my sleep, I look at car doors closing and I think that I will see fingers caught in them, I am afraid that that same voice will be heard."

"And what does all of this have to do with the cat's tail?" asked the short guy.

"Maybe he is shifting the issue to the cat so that he can relive a similar event without taking responsibility," said the supervisor. "It's one thing for a cat to shriek and another for a human to do it. It's a well-known operation. What we are more interested in is the method, the way the tail was cut off."

"We are only interested in the way," said the short guy. "This will immediately go in the archive, it will not go into your file. Say it in a general and abstract manner, like a recipe."

"Title: How to cut off a cat's tail," replied the supervisor while the tape was recording.

"We open all of the doors," I began, "as well as the windows of the house. We remove the doorstop, if there is one, from the front door or from any other door of equal weight. We place a cat treat at a normal distance from the door, preferably fish, and we arrange for the cat's tail to be stuffed in the door of our choosing while petting it and as the cat is devoted to eating the treat, or something similar. We eventually let the door slam, taking advantage of the drafts which have been created in the house from the open doors and windows, but only after we have also pushed the door quite a bit."

"So basically it was the draft," concluded the short guy, and his supervisor gestured for him to be quiet by pointing out the tape recorder. I continued:

"The cat does not stick around for us to administer first aid, and because the doors and windows are open, it jumps out screaming and disappears. Don't be afraid. Because the cat is bonded with the house, it returns the next day and walks around the rooms without a tail and you can present it as a rare breed to your guests."

"Amazing," said the short guy. "Can you imagine?"

"It doesn't seem to me that these two stories tie in well with each other," said the supervisor, "it's like they have gaps somewhere and are not completed. Something is missing, and something important at that. We cannot excuse the cruel shift toward the cats. You could have made amends to the child by buying candy or taking it to the botanical gardens so that he could look at the fish. Why didn't you immediately redeem yourself for the wickedness you inflicted on the child?"

"It didn't exist anymore. He died a few days later."

"There is the gap. Now we can somewhat explain things. How did the child die?"

"What killed the child?" the short guy asked fiercely.

"The child. The child." said the woman lifelessly.

"Gastrointestinal problems."

"And you didn't take him to a doctor?" asked the woman in a disconcerted way.

"When my mother went to the hospital it was too late. The child always had a sensitive stomach, and a woman from the neighborhood fed him legumes and made him sick. The child lasted three, barely four days and then he died.

"""Why did you bring me the child now, madam?" asked the doctor. "He's almost dead."" She carried the dead child in her arms. The whole way there her hair was undone, she even lost one of her slippers. It was the Occupation, there were no taxis, there was no money for taxis.

It was Monday, and I didn't know anything, I was selling kouloúria in the city center, I hadn't suspected anything, do you believe me? I couldn't have predicted it, isn't that right? I was selling kouloúria downtown. We were a gang, and when we finished selling the kouloúria, we went for a dip at the lake in the botanical gardens. And I didn't even understand how he died, nor did I believe it when, coming home at late noon, I heard crying and saw the top of the casket propped up against the door. They were waiting for me to cover the body, he was ochre in color and his eyes were closed. They lifted him and broke an urn behind him. My mother was screaming and broke down from thereon out. He was a sweet and very smart child, he was our lastborn, he would have made something of himself, we would have all helped with his studies, we'd all be grown by then, the war would be over, he would have been the best of us. Father sat silently in the corner for days."

The tape recorded everything, the woman was hunched over her papers, she was searching for something again, the short guy was somewhat unsettled, and the supervisor got up to take a walk, maybe to stretch his limbs. He reached the edge of the plateau that was still illuminated and then came back.

"Will we continue?" asked the woman.

"The case has not concluded. He is hiding something from us again. He presents himself as completely devoid of fault. What did you do on Sunday?"

"On Sunday… On Sunday…" I said as if contemplating, and then: "I don't remember."

He signaled at the short guy who then moved in a nonchalant way, as if he was coming toward me, and at the same time the supervisor asked:

"You didn't see the child on Sunday?"

"I hastily came back inside for a moment. He was laying in his swing. "How are you?" I asked him. "My tummy hurts," he responded lifelessly. I left because I was in a hurry and no suspicions ran through my mind."

"Why were you in a hurry? Why did you only go back inside for a little bit?"

I faltered. The short guy has stopped half way through. He started to slowly go up again behind the woman's desk. She gestured for me to keep going.

"I think I had a rented bicycle. Time was running out and I had to move on."

"So, he had money."

"Do you know how much extra cash all those people made selling kouloúria?" said the short guy who was coming back down to return to his seat.

"Did you have money?" asked the woman aggressively.

"I did." I admitted.

"Was it enough to cover the doctor's payment?"

"It was."

"If you hadn't rented the bike and instead used that money to take the child to the doctor, would the child have been saved?"

"I thought about that afterward, the moment when they lifted him and the urn broke behind him, and later as I watched my silent father, as my mother cried, that thought poisoned me, I felt responsible for this death, and it is the only death I experienced so intensely."

"How old were you?"

"Not more than ten, and since then I've felt old, like my life became irreparably twisted forever, this death marked me and everything else came distorted."

"Alright," said the supervisor in a satisfied way. Then, in an attempt to temper the impression: "This happens to most people, they try to regulate themselves because they didn't take the sick person to the doctor, or they didn't take them immediately, or in the end that they didn't take them to someone better—

something will occur to make this responsibility return to them. The thing is, though, that they keep it secret, but it's okay, because when the moment comes with the right method they air out everything."

SUPERVISOR : Where were you born?

X. : In the big city, but on the margin, in the squatty houses, brick and mortars and shacks, close to the sandlot. The roads had a dark color, and there were many alleys and it was dark everywhere. In the early years I used to hide in the alcoves, I used to disappear all the time playing hide and seek.

SUPERVISOR : They would eventually find you.

X. : Correct, they found me, they'd tag me and I had to run after them and reveal myself so that I'd have enough time to tag them first, I had to do to them whatever they did to me, it couldn't be any other way, and when I was seeking I was forced to bring each one of them into the light. One time I hid behind some barrels full of tar. "I will sit here as if I don't exist," I thought and held my breath. I was never going to be revealed, and in fact I had started to get sleepy, when I heard the voices of the others, "help," desperate voice which pierced your ears, "freedom for everyone." I couldn't remain in nonexistence. I left my hiding spot and ran in case I could save others from being tagged.

SUPERVISOR : The right thing to do.

X. : That's how I used to do things back then. I ran for the freedom of others, and when someone was wronged, I always put myself in the middle. Of course they'd bruise up my head, I went to jail, I was tormented.

SUPERVISOR : You don't talk about your house.

X. : It was just one room and when I opened the door I'd immediately find myself on the street. It was like there wasn't a house, the walls were thin and you could hear what people were saying on the other side, they'd argue, you could even hear the grunts they made in their sleep. I would play outside on the street all day and I would only come back inside at night to go to bed. I tell you all this so that you can understand that my home did not set me up for who I became, good, bad, it was the neighborhood and quarter, especially when the war and famine arrived. I was responsible for our rations and people would steal my spot all the time, others wormed their way in front of me and I was forced to worm my way further up, there was constant bickering which would come to a head by the people who shoved the most. I learned to struggle and put pressure because others were pressuring too, I wronged because others did it too. Then things became more wild with all the killings.

SUPERVISOR : You can speak freely. We do not pick sides.

X. : I know.

SUPERVISOR : Whose side were you on?

X. : With our guys. The first killing I witnessed was a kid two or three years older than me, his skull was cracked open and his brains were spilt on the dirt. I swore to crack open the skull of a guy on the other side when I was old enough. I later saw a partisan lying supine in the middle of the road, it was like they had dragged him from the bed, he was wearing a striped tank top and woolen long johns. I saw him again in the morning all rigid, just before they were about to lift him and toss him in the car.

SUPERVISOR : Did you approve?

X. : Maybe, because I thought to myself "he got what he deserved," as if he was the one who cracked the kid's skull open and now he was paying for it. After, I saw many more killings and I slowly ceased feeling sorrow for our guys, and neither did I feel a wild happiness for the deaths of our opponents. They were simply dead men who filled me up and nothing made an impression on me anymore, and most importantly I did not care which faction they belonged to, nor did I care about the hangings in the small square, I only remember the tilt of their heads, they all leaned forward a bit, some to the left and some to the right, and I can still see that guy's mucus that had ran from his nose and had frozen like a piece of pasta, two or three inches from his nostril. Same thing with the paralyzed girl's body after the fire in the shacks. The others sparked the fire and people flew out.

He rubbed his eyes a little bit, he looked tired and he sat down on the chair. He then took a folder into his purview.

"You said that your life had been marked since then, that you feel fatigued, is that right?"

"Yes, that's what I said."

"But these papers here present an active man, a happy one, a man sure of himself, with social hobbies, how do these things reconcile with each other?"

"We have another report which depicts him in exactly the opposite way," said the woman.

"What kind of reports do they make," mumbled the short guy.

"In any case, the original category would not be applicable," continued the woman without paying mind to the short guy's interruption, "if we admitted that he was satisfied with his life."

"He is probably a contrarian," concluded the supervisor.

"He was concealing himself. He would present himself one way, when in reality he was another way," said the short guy. "You can't imagine how sneaky some people are. Just like that old man from the other day who pinched my leg that still hurts me."

"He didn't come of his own will," said the woman. "He

denied everything up until the end, and the final judgment was delivered in the presence of witnesses."

"This guy will take back his testimonies at the end, just wait and see," insisted the short guy, "we will need witnesses and he will take up our entire evening, just watch."

"You will be paid overtime," the supervisor intervened. "But I don't believe that he will retract them. Everything, school, marriage, his general integration, even his imprisonment happened with his consent, isn't that right?" he turned to me.

"How is that possible?" I complained. "It's a well known fact that, for jail at least, they send you there against your will, regardless of whether or not you are guilty."

"Didn't I say this would happen?" the short guy complained.

"Nevertheless. You still showed up on your own, you sat on the bench, they needed your deposition, because when they asked if you are guilty or not, you didn't give an answer and this meant that you didn't care about any sort of verdict, right? If you didn't want to go to jail, you would have said not guilty, right?"

"But I didn't say I was."

"This is the double standard of your character. Always between the two poles. You preferred prison, and you did this pathetically. You did not defend your ideas, you didn't even cuss out your judges."

X. : That is also a position to take.

SHORT GUY : A gutless one.

THE WOMAN : You did not exit that place as a hero.

SHORT GUY : You came out a wimp.

X. : Scared, but not broken.

SUPERVISOR : And why did you break down later?

THE WOMAN : Who pressured you and caused you to break?

SHORT GUY : Don't say that they put a knife to your throat.

SUPERVISOR : Even if that happened, you should have endured it.

SHORT GUY : But nothing like that happened, did it?

X. : No.

SHORT GUY : Do you see?

SUPERVISOR : You changed on your own, right?

THE WOMAN : He is dazed now, he doesn't know what he wants.

SHORT GUY : He sits in prison all these years, he is deprived of things, he endures it, and when he gets out, he decides to change.

SUPERVISOR : What do you think this place is, do you believe that anyone can change at any time they like, that they can leap from one situation to the next? Are ideas like shirts?

SHORT GUY : Everyone is destined to their own fate. A clerk until the end. How will we institute order when everyone changes? How will the others sort things out?

SUPERVISOR : He does not accept any order, not even order in the universe.

THE WOMAN : He is so volatile. Can we maybe base our opinions on this side of his personality and return him?

SHORT GUY : No way.

SUPERVISOR : I wish, but it is impossible. This guy did not change to join the others, he exited the game completely. He does not accept any rule. Do you want proof? (Addressing X.) Have you gone out of bounds?

X. : Certainly.

SUPERVISOR : Did you see the difference between the sheep? The ones over there are branded, they've burned numbers on them with hot metal. The ones over here are free.

X. : It's true, they don't have marks on them, but a shepherd guards them.

SUPERVISOR : Anyway, whose side are you on, the ones over here or the ones over there?

X. : I'm on the side of the sheep.

SUPERVISOR : Do you see?

THE WOMAN : Now you've left us speechless. No one should defend you. You do not want to be saved.

SHORT GUY : He's humorous on top of everything.

THE WOMAN : Your life is one continuous mistake and you do

not make any effort, at least in the last moment, to change your circumstance, to fix something. It's like you are pursuing your demise.

SHORT GUY : Don't waste your time with this son of a bitch, he has gone completely astray with those cats, the dogs, the child, and other things which will potentially come to light in a little while.

SUPERVISOR : Just like the case of spousal desertion.

THE WOMAN : He has things like that against him too?

SHORT GUY : He skipped out on the house he shared with his wife and now you're keeping him away from me?

SUPERVISOR : He left with another woman. I can't say much, we're men, we might like another woman, but that does not mean that we should lock up our houses. Go with the other woman, have fun, and come back home at night holding a bouquet or a box of sweets, preferably pastries, kiss your wife, tell her some sweet words, and everything will be okay.

SHORT GUY : Of course. Don't wreck your home.

THE WOMAN : You can even pluck your eyes out, but at least come back home afterward.

SUPERVISOR : When the other woman is also married, then two homes are wrecked.

THE WOMAN : And you must have been old enough, I mean you must have formed some morals.

SUPERVISOR : It is not a moral problem. His conscience is like rubber which he immediately adjusts.
SHORT GUY : This guy? He changes morals in an instant and slips.
THE WOMAN : Then, why are we examining him?
SUPERVISOR : He himself will tell us what is torturing him about this situation. Here, you may speak. Tape recorder.

Everything inside of me was blurry. I pressured myself and the images started to arrive one by one, most of them irrelevant, and only the ones that concerned her husband made me shiver, I felt the need to talk about him.

"He was wearing a tank top and was laying down on dirty, wrinkly sheets on the divan, his eyes were blue and shining, and I was wandering from room to room, I was smelling blood, the coming storm, an attempted suicide, but not to prevent it, but to live it, I paced inside the room waiting for the moment his eyes dimmed."

"He was laying on a low divan, a cheap mattress with exposed stuffing, his head rested just beyond the pillows, he was begging me to find her and bring her back to him, she was stolen, a fugitive because of me, I remember his eyes like a dog's eyes watching me trustfully, and I discouraged him, I repeatedly took his hope away, "she is not going to come back," I told him, I hustled him by asking to see his veins spatter the sheets and walls, and for that dark colored stuffing to ravenously soak up the blood."

"He was laying down on sweat soaked sheets, and every now and then something came out of him like a sigh and litany for the dead, My Love, and I felt a chill pass through my body as I heard him mumble "I will kill him, whoever it is," I then took him to the furthest bounds of suspicion and returned him afterward to that dog-like gaze of trust, I even came to feel his fists on my face, and subsequently the caress of his eyes. He was a young man with arms made of steel who automatically transformed them to Chasteberry trees."

"The next day he attempted suicide, just like I had predicted. I wasn't there and others saved him. I didn't meet him again after that. He left, he didn't leave a trace, maybe he immigrated or remarried, I don't know exactly, but in any case he did not get back together with her. We lived together for a little while and then broke up, I don't remember the reason why, or the deeper causes, but I later thought that it might have been because of the lack of danger, and the fact is that I had an intense desire to return to my wife. I abandoned her in the middle of the road, just like I had left my wife a few months prior, saying the same words: "I don't want to do this anymore," or "I can't do this anymore," this was the overall meaning of my words, and she started crying, in fact, I gave her my handkerchief to wipe herself, I left it in her hands and went away."

"Son of a bitch," said the short guy between his teeth while turning off the tape recorder.

"He is a total scumbag," said the supervisor.

The woman took two needles out of a drawer and started knitting. The ball of yarn was not in sight, she might have tossed it in the trash can so that it wouldn't roll around. The other two immediately jumped on me and asked various questions, and at the beginning I tried to give a couple of answers, but realized that it was in vain and gave up. I had already made my decisions, that is why I let them say and ask the same things over and over.

- Why is there a why?[18]

- I don't understand you. Why is there a why?

- I asked, why the cat.

- Oh, the cat.

- Why should we have forgotten about the cat?

- But why bring up the cat again?

- Of course we should. Didn't you cut its tail off?

- Why are you making the stars out to be at fault and then you get upset with them?

- You don't accept any order, okay?

---

18. Translator's note: The word "why" in Greek sounds like the word for cat.

- Please explain to us how you were able to transform a simple case of cryptic tonsillitis into surreptitiousness?

- Can't the same thing happen with a case of cryptorchidism?

- Anyway, will you ever speak again?

- Did you know that you could die any moment now and we might never find out anything in the end?

- Cryptic.

- Secretive.

- Agent.

- Lackey.

- Of Lacedaemon.

- Demon.

- You destroyed the world order. What did the universe do to you and now you're upset with it?

- Why do you ridicule language?

-What is the relationship between boutique and boútia?

- Why do you constantly confuse these two words in your writing? Why do you correlate them?[19]

- So you think you can become a star, don't you?

- Well, in what way will you become a star?

- By putting phosphorus underneath the skin? You can't be serious.

---

19. Translator's note: The word "boútia," meaning thighs, alliterates with "boutique."

– And not only that, but you'll stand further above the stars because you can say the words tsilibíki and Miss Bitzídou, right?

– Is this proper conduct?

– No, tell me, is this serious behavior?

– And is it still in your hands to regulate the behavior of cells?

– Do you think others will be indifferent just because you are?

– You need to put in effort right until the end, even if it is fruitless.

– Why do you let yourself go? You can already see that things are not panning out for you, so why are you smoking?

– Since when did you acquire this conceit? We want an answer.

I was submerged in my own thoughts and didn't understand how they expected an answer from me. The woman was knitting. The other two looked at me worriedly.

"We asked you," said the supervisor, "and you owe us an answer."

"What exactly?"

"Since when did you acquire this conceit?"

"Since I became ill on the inside."

"How did this illness manifest?"

"My pinkie suddenly started to swell. I didn't pay attention to it, I thought it might have been a bug bite, but it kept growing, it became enormous and transferred to the other fingers, and slowly but surely to the other limbs, everything became massive, but despite this I was able to fit through doors, I sat in the same chair and slept in the same bed."

"He can't be saved," muttered the woman.

"What other symptoms did you have?" asked the supervisor.

"I lived on a main boulevard, and as I was laying down, the cars would cross over my forehead, I listened to the thrum of their engines begin from the left temple and then simultaneously all the way on the right, but the sounds became confused in the middle and I couldn't distinguish their directions. Only the motorcycles stubbornly crossed the entire distance, they'd pin themselves over my eyebrows for a moment and then leave in the opposite direction. Thankfully these motorcycles existed and broke through the permanent buzzing inside of me so that I could discern some unique event."

"The thing that scared me was my cheek which extended itself all the way to the corner, it dragged itself on the asphalt seeking a gentle hand to lift it up, just like dough that had been risen too much, this sensation upset me, and my hair was in danger of getting caught in the trees when it was windy, I was afraid that it would get stuck in the sap or that I'd get caught in the thorns of an acacia."

"Further in, I couldn't exactly tell what was going on. I did hear my intestines making noise though, just like the train which crosses the bridge, my chest was like a boiling pot, and whenever I hocked a loogie, it sounded like an explosion at the quarry, I saw it fall from very high up toward the sea, and all those things that people thought were foam and waves, primarily those who flew on airplanes and looked down, were actually my own loogies which I disseminated just like Perrault's Little Thumb, they were marks for my return and they weren't at danger of anyone cleaning them up, the foam and waves will always be there to show me my way."

"Were there people who accepted this side of you?" asked one of the two.

"That didn't concern me. Regardless, I didn't show it off, I hid it deep inside of me, and my actions still remained, at least for the others, they were small ones, within human reason. I smoked cigarettes, drank water, and from time to time I'd chase a fly if it bothered me too much. Nevertheless, it seems that only I was aware of this gigantism, because whenever I tried to uproot a tree, I would eventually just manage to break off a small branch. Generally speaking the objects around me retained the same disposition toward me as they did before. My suit, for example, was a little wide and my shoes, just like usual, made my calluses hurt."

SUPERVISOR : He has gone completely out of bounds.
SHORT GUY : I realized it from the very first moment, nothing will change with this guy.
SUPERVISOR : Unfortunately, there is no salvation. This divisiveness of his, the bipolarity of his character.
SHORT GUY : He's a scumbag, what did you expect?
SUPERVISOR : He is burdened with a thousand and one weaknesses.
X. : That's my business.
SUPERVISOR : Since when is it your business?
X. : I can put an end to this matter on my own. My will is just enough to do this.
SUPERVISOR : Again with your will?
SHORT GUY : Do you forget that you surrendered everything, razors, nail clipper, other sharp objects?
SUPERVISOR : And, really, I doubt that you have the will to do such a thing.
SHORT GUY : Why don't you relegate yourself to us, who, in any case, operate legally?

SUPERVISOR : There isn't another way, anyhow.

X. : Then, which will of mine are you blabbering about?

SUPERVISOR : Compose yourself.

SHORT GUY : Let's say that this is your will.

SUPERVISOR : It will happen either way, so why are you putting up a fight?

SHORT GUY : It will happen in the most painless way.

X. : Which way?

SHORT GUY : You can choose. We recommend electrical shock, it only lasts for a few seconds, you won't even realize it's happening.

SUPERVISOR : As long as you compose yourself.

SHORT GUY : You don't need to move. Everything will happen where you are. The bench is connected to the electricity. I just need to plug it in. A few spasms and everything will be over. Please do not pick another method, it would be troublesome and it's late already, we need to go home.

X. : What time is it?

SHORT GUY : Thirty past four on the dot. Almost everyone prefers the method we recommend to them.

X. : Day or night?

SHORT GUY : Early in the morning. You would make it easier for us, and you wouldn't lose anything.

SHORT GUY : Disgusting. You will only feel the first spasm,

maybe the second one. Don't feel ambivalent anymore, you made the decision. Should I plug it in?
X. : Alright.

The woman gathered her knit and placed it in the drawer. Then, holding her jacket with one hand, she went down to her supervisor's plateau. He showed her a document and the woman signed it. The short guy also passed through the supervisor's plateau so that he could jot down his mark, and he then went to a corner and started battling with some cables. A bright light shone down on me. I felt the first spasm, the second followed shortly after, then the third...

Ρετάλια
Worthless Men

TSILIBIK OR TSILIBAKI

It's an alteration of Kant's well-known opinions— "I can't, I can't"[20] —not a lexical one, but a more substantial one which determines my ultimate attitude, something like a mockery of the stars, a continual relegation of celestial bodies and a kind of confusion with human ones, even with the entirety of the social organism.

Kant admired the harmony of the sky, but I think about the same space in a completely different way: How solid is the firmament? Does it freak out as much as I do these wintry nights? Does it suffer from loneliness and a lack of meaning?

There are two things that always make me wonder: The bewilderment within me and the pointlessness of the stars crowding the sky together, what are they doing there? A dim light and decoration which is needless most times. In the same way they didn't crash into Kant, we don't know what happened in the past, nor do we know what will happen in the future. Anyway, people have managed to not collide with moving bodies, it's a question of traffic regulation by electronic brains and, at least for me, this doesn't matter at all, it does not excite me in the slightest.

---

20. *Translator's note: Chakkas wrote these words in English.*

At the end of the day being a star is not something exceptional. I can completely turn into light by tossing a certain amount of phosphorus in my veins, my ganglia, and even underneath my skin. I will not only be a flaming bramble, I will be a moving one, too. Not like those damn fires that are extinguished by the first little cloud that passes in front of them, or being extinguished by the fluttering of my eyes. I am way above the stars. I can say "Hello, mister Oulkéroglоú," or "How do you do, Missus Bitzídou." I can even say "tsilibík,"[21] whereas all the stars can't even say "tsil."

And the harmony that exists inside and outside of us does not matter to me. I have had enough of harmonies, stuff like car-star and wife-knife make me want to puke, but disharmony delights me, let stars-dicks be even if the words don't match, let us disharmonize once in a while, easy rhyme schemes have burdened us enough already, the cries of electric bouzoúkia, the boîtes and boutiques have nothing to do with boútia. I prefer the return to the source, to the crevice, the maidenhair ferns weep and the satyrs pull them aside, dripping, and make way for me to reach the root.

Athens, your harmony lies in shopping and being cocky at the same time. You auction everything from seas to islands, be-

21. *Translator's note: Nonsense word.*

ginning with the lowest bid. I am also selling my youth so that I can save myself from the city of sell-outs, I will give one of my testicles for two black eyes, eight hours of my life for one button-up shirt, my poems carcasses for the ignorant, my quivering heart sowing eternal light.

And how do you think Hesperus is doing? He is trembling in agony, perhaps realizing that his end is near, and he begs for help that he knows will never come. He is the first of all the stars to appear in the night sky and call out with no response, why does he prolong his agony?Let them finally collide with each other and for this affair to reach a conclusion that will convey to me something about this universal convergence.

For, it is true, it has been a long time since I have been emotionally moved, I am almost empty and it is necessary for me for the universe to become a mess in a way that mirrors my internal one: Comets that have escaped their orbit and move menacingly close to us with their tails, first-rate stars that are lost in infinity and other nonexistent ones that take their place, Sagittarius finally shooting his arrow, and Aquarius' endless well spilling forth like a tumble of blonde hair, just like a waterfall which disappears into a sinkhole, pouring out of the chaos of the world.

Science and sociological interpretation have tired me. I seek a society in which everything will become a mess: A-list stars playing the roles of extras, protesters and tanks in the streets, who's first, who's second, everyone pretending to preside over the eschaton (then they will tell you I was just carrying out orders, boss), small folk who use the bus to travel, Prime Ministers who wait in line at the station.

I don't like perfect societies, aesthetics, and harmonies. They all suffer in some way, bodies, the universe and groups against the cliff, moreover, there is no appetite for a new set-up. Instead, there is a mania for more destruction. Anyway, the ones who say that they are building a government, the priests, the mysteries, are only wreaking more havoc.

Expediency and logic do not interest me anymore, especially the inevitable death of some of my cells, of some of the organisms that are coming full circle and that will not return. Even in my own body I want my cells to fight, the old ones to persist, to resist, the dead ones to no longer be eliminated, I want for them to remain there, causing chaos.

OF MY OWN FREE WILL

I went to jail of my own free will. They were the so-called heroic years then, and maybe some family traditions contributed, because when I was born my grandmother had wished for me to be a "captain of the mountains," and my mother lulled me to sleep with Aretousa's song. (Even in the first verses there were "sad tidings" and "exiles".) All of these contributed to my internment.

Naturally, the decision was made by some agrilokoús (in my pig-latin meaning old bastards), who from their high benches looked at me like I was a fly, and maybe it was revenge for my youth, but I admit that my body wanted it a little bit, my blood was drawn to it, so to speak.

However, regardless of whether or not my body was drawn to it, those bastards did not act in good faith by handing out the sentences as if they were kouloúria. They haven't lived a day in there, or else they would think twice before giving ten, fifteen, and twenty year sentences. Now that I think about it, if the opportunity ever rises, I will send them to prison for six months, not much more, because they are not at fault for anything, but I want them to understand what it means to be sentenced, and then I will place them at their benches again so that I can joke about how they will deem everyone innocent. Of course, this is impossible, because they are shitty old bastards, and one by one they die off and clean the place up, and my situation is still slow-going, it might never arrive since I made it so difficult and demanding, I don't have fans anymore and the last person I admitted my plan to suggested that we yank them a little by their ties.

The thing that enrages me the most is that they succeeded in not making me cuss them out. I regretted it from the first moment, of course, and that is perhaps why I am worsening things now, since I acted decently at the time. Others dragged them in the courtroom, just like that one who had to carry three consecutive death sentences on his back and instead of saying thank-you to them he told them to take his ball sack after the third execution and to turn them into a tobacco pouch, unless they hadn't already been pierced by bullets that is. Those were heroic years back then and I thought that it was honorable of me to sleep in the switchgear rooms beside thirty-centimeter long rats. At first I looked very happy and was always smiling at the others, sometimes I even smiled at the walls, even at the guards, until the moment someone slapped me because he thought that I was making fun of him. After this incident, whenever I attempted to smile, a freakish grimace would appear and my face turned to stone as time passed. The era of naivety was definitely over.

Many times I had the urge to grab onto the bars and yell "get me out, hey, my will has changed now," but they insisted that I needed to insist on the original will, they even had agents among us who said "it's not right for anyone to change." That's when I saw the guy with the three death sentences apply for clemency and beg, he wrote to his family to see if they could delay his sentence until the great evil had passed, I saw him tremble once the guards opened the prison doors, even if they were simply handing out letters. They started to set up along the wall.

I only hung out with the most desperate, with those who narrowly walked in the opposite direction in the courtyard. They didn't care about the newspaper, nor did they belong to the group, it was a question of whether there were other people around them. I approached them to figure out if they were still here of their own free will. I was never able to solve these cases.

Only George, the single madman, was the one I discovered who stayed of his own volition. He would take me to the center of the courtyard and we would talk in a hushed manner, because there were radars all around the prison and we were being spied on, every night our enemies would bombard our cells with cobalt, and this is why we'd exit them like fainting chickens in the morning, it was not only because of the lack of air. In the center of the courtyard there was the pine tree. It was there that we would tie ourselves up with an imaginary rope and walk around like horses at the threshing. George was on the outer part, he limped a little bit to match my stride and slowly started pushing me toward the tree, each round I lost a few centimeters, until at the end the circle got so small that I was forced to bump into the tree. That's when he would develop his theories about carrots. Cobalt, radars, x-rays, all things that were unleashed by dark forces were neutralized by carrots, and he would take out a carrot from a dirty pocket in his military jacket, he would munch on it, he wanted to offer me some, but I always declined, he resented the fact that I mistrusted him even after all of his guidance, and many times I caught him ready to push me up against the tree, he wanted to lynch me there, his eyes flickered with rage, but what else could I do since I wasn't convinced of his theories, only one thought remained in my mind, which I dared to ask him one time: "What will happen when it's not carrot season?". He looked at me suspiciously and said: "You are also a miner." That's what he called people who undermined the unity of the prison, and he cast me aside.

It was for the best. "I reached a wall" at the well and made my strolls as long as I could, always far away from the dangerous tree, alone, so very alone, I didn't want any more theories, analyses and opinions, I didn't want anything, I only counted the days, months and years, and scaled the wall little by little until I made it to the rim. A slice of sea, a glass of salt, bitterness at the roof of my mouth. The doors to the houses are small, and they all open inward, a divan with a woman laying on it, next to her a flock of singing birds. The world is beautiful. I will stand here to gaze at it for a bit with my luggage in hand, within it many years and some books. This is my will now, to look at homes, seas, and mountains.

The next time they told me to enter again of my own free will I told them that I couldn't. "But, why, you are one of them," insisted the guys above me, "you are one of us," said the guys beneath me. "I am no one's. Finally, I am my own."

IN FRONT OF A GRAVE

I went to Marx's grave. To get there, I crossed through a park with two ponds and saw a little squirrel and offered it some chocolate. The squirrel took it using its front paws and munched. Then, I went to the cemetery. When I was in jail I received a package that had some chocolates inside. Of course, I shared them with my friends. Later, when I got into an argument with another inmate, he hit back at me saying: "You didn't give me a chocolate." He was a mountain man for life. A few days later he made a statement and left. The cemetery's old, abandoned. The Jewish headstones in the distance are even more abandoned. His stands out. It's a large granite head. He wrote "Das Kapital," loved his wife, and was bankrolled by Friedrich. In the year 2000, there will be millions of adulterers. In 2000, "Das Kapital" will finally be translated correctly (not the dissemination of the product), anyone will be able to appreciate its nerve and irony. I chew on my chocolate and look at him. Usually people leave wreaths or plant bombs. I whistle the song "Oh! Carol". I have to pee. Desert. I move a little bit to the side and piss into a hedge. The squirrel comes out, it looks like the park and cemetery communicate, and with its front paws he gestures to me that the chocolate has run out. "Listen, rat, if you even are the same thing, I am not giving you chocolate. These things need to be split up evenly. You can't take advantage of our acquaintance." I once shared this rare prison food only with my friends, and as a result that other guy made a statement. It took me some night before I was able to sleep again. Because of me, Marx lost a fan and now that I am standing in front of his grave I don't want something similar to happen again. I'm sleeping well.

Besides, I made a statement too, but not because they didn't give me chocolate, it was due to other reasons. There was some guy who was used to saying "Vladimir said," and because he was the one who said it, the rest of us had to abide. I mainly didn't like that he called him Vladimir, as if they were first cousins. Another called him Ilyich. They rarely talked about Karl, and even more rarely about Friedrich. But, they still liked saying the phrase "let the dead go on,"[22] that someone coined afterward. All those guys who came afterward said bullshit. I loved Vladimir, Vladimir with the naughty cowlick that imprinted itself "with a sledgehammer to the world's cranium,"[23] maybe because he was suspicious early on, maybe because of the bullet that wedged itself in his cranium.

Everything began with that granite head that stands in front of me, these guys and the others, then those guys and the

---

22. *Translator's note: This quote is a reference to Joseph Stalin.*

23. *Translator's note: Chakkas is drawing from Giannis Ritsos' translation of Vladimir Mayakovsky's "Cloud with Trousers".*

guys after, the good and the bad, but the good got out of the middle quickly, all of the Dzhugashvilis clamored and wiped out everyone, and only the unpalatable ones remained. You will tell me "find me a pot that can boil milk without it spilling over." This is what I have been attempting all of these years, every morning I tell myself to be careful so that it doesn't boil over and I always fail. This is how we all failed, maybe Marx himself too, because I don't believe he wanted those unpalatable people around.

AN UNCLE

And both siblings were involved in the same matter; Vasílis did not have a death sentence and begged Sávvas to make a statement so that he could make it out alive. Unturning head. Many years after the execution Vasílis finally signed, got out, got married, and baptized his first child Sávva. He then married his sister off, and they named their first boy Sávva. Then, his little brother got married, he had a girl, and when they tried for a second child, it also turned out to be a girl. The third time was the charm and they named the child Sávva, too. It was not that Vasílis wanted his child and his sibling's children to be similar to that unturned head or for them to continue the way he did. Even now, he shudders at the thought that they might get into trouble as they grow up, although Vasílis was never one to be a coward, his little heart told him so when he was young and that is how he got himself tangled up in that matter, in fact, he recommended to Sávva to make a statement so that he could save himself, and he would hold out until the end. You'd say that he didn't have his neck on the line. But, ten to fifteen years in the hole is no small sacrifice. Sávvas should have listened to his advice even though he was younger than him. "Hey, think of our father, our mother's sorrow." He went straight to the firing squad without taking anyone into account.

Now, Vasílis only concerns himself with work and the house. The name Sávvas does not ring a bell and spares him of hurt. Now, Sávvas is the new kid who comes in and out of the house, tosses his book bag on the bed and asks for pocket money for movies and souvláki, and Vasílis' only worry is about him getting involved with bad crowds. New troubles. The other Sávvas is forgotten. There is, however, his magnified picture in the nice room and when his kid's friends ask "who is that man?", the new Sávvas gives a short answer without much explanation. The younger kids say he is "an uncle," and don't know anything. Why would Vasílis open up old wounds now? If the kids want to know when they are older, no one will forbid them from knowing.

But the ones who killed Sávvas refuse to forget him and every now and then they bother Vasílis, they call him about "his case," they impose questions, they can't believe that Vasílis has forgotten. "We killed his brother," they think, " how can this ever be forgotten?" Vasílis becomes irritated with these things and the fact that they don't leave him alone to do his job, to concern himself with his kids and nieces and nephews. "Even if I tell them, Mários, that I have forgotten it, which I won't ever tell them, but if I did, they still would not believe me. They are afraid. It seems that this is the only thing that occupies their minds. It's better that way. I, for one, sleep soundly."

KAISARIANI'S SHOOTING RANGE

They say that the blood running from the car was covered by the arm of some patriot holding carnations. Years later, legends will emerge that the asphalt sprouted flowers, the same ones that might have been placed on those dark spots. And old women may tell this story to their grandchildren, like a fairy tale, they will say that some night in May the street almost looked like a field of poppies.

All these are fictions and transgressions. The truth is that the blood was left to dry all over the place, until the rain washed it away, but only on the asphalt, because beyond the big gate there was a dirt road that sucked it up, the blood became one with the dust and left no trace.

And even today there is nothing to remind us of these executions. Only some scribbles remained on the corner of the avenue next to the range, the ones that attempted to cover letters that had been written by others during the first months of the liberation. In red paint they wrote "Slaughterhouse Avenue." Everything had faded, blue scribbles with letters underneath, they all slowly disappeared, both red and blue, and only a faded new color which was the product of those two was discernible, perhaps indicating a suspicion about what happened, about what was going to happen, about what ultimately did not happen. On one side some symbols attempted to exist, on the other there was the wilful intent to become erased forever, for the space to not remind us of anything, the passing years generated this bastard colorful smudge, a common street without a face, like so many streets in Kaisarianí, like the thousands of streets in Athens.

And yet from those events certain secret symbols still exist that cannot be fabricated, they escape the persistent efforts of some people to bury and conceal everything, they are secret symbols that can be detected by a trained eye: They are the frightened birds that flee the forest, they flit in flocks as if startled by secret gusts of wind. There are the cypresses which cannot hold on to their fruit, the blood jumps from the roots toward the shoots and the cones fall to the ground. It's the subterranean blood.

And there is the wind which swirls trash around, yellowed letters from another area, a cigarette's rolling paper with the words "I am leaving, my eyes turned to…" (the other words faded), a damaged newsboy cap with a substance on its torn lining, a piece of underwear with dried semen, "my beloved woman" written with a black pencil, and other scraps of paper "my son," "my siblings," "comrades".

They are still there, on Shooting Range Avenue, and they all get tangled up between the legs of an unsuspecting pedestrian, who then tries to get rid of them with a kick, they chase him down to the corner, he turns and disappears. Then, the garbageman passes by with his cart: "Why did they send me here? The road is unsullied." The road is clean. The dust devil lifted the scraps of paper very high above the roofs. But the time will come again when they will fall at the pedestrian's feet and he will curse the mayor for not sending someone to pick up the garbage, the trash will come again, because the messages must reach their destination sometime, even if they are thirty or forty years late, even if they are old and forgotten, their recipients dead, they must go, because who is the one who will be able to bear hearing the complaint:
"I was executed. I decomposed in a mass grave, they poured asbestos, they buried others on top of me, I became nutritious soil, I became only a memory that slowly faded alongside my mother's life, but that piece of paper I tossed onto the street needs to be picked up sometime so that it doesn't wander around like a stray. Justice."

The city council is in session. The topic is the worship of the dead, memorials, kóllyva[24] and priests. The latter suggest a modest ceremony with an archimandrite (but not with a despot), the latter, stepping firmly onto holy bones, passionately demand a despot at all costs, a grand ceremony in the church, the laying of wreaths at the site of the executions, an overseers of the ceremonies, helpers and other organizers who will regulate the program, dances, recitations, songs, and parades.

Of course the majority has been secured and the decision has been made in the "joint," the general directions have been given from "below," everything is arranged by the party, they know who will cry and when, with what they will say and in what kind of voice. The council meeting is entirely formal, no speech will change the agenda, no suggestion will be heard, no matter how wise it is. However, there are those council members who take the floor and then there are those who suspect that they do not have an official role on the day of the celebration, they now rush to say something about "the dead," so that they can be seen by the few listeners of the city council.

I receive a note from a colleague who is somewhat partial to my

24. Translator's note: Boiled wheat served at funerals.

opinions. "How long will this mindless chatter go on?" I want to answer him on the same piece of paper: "What will happen with the exploitation of the dead every year?" I end up turning the note into an airplane and while the chatter continues on with the occasional agonous cries of "our dead," I am tempted to to shoot it onto the bald spat of a random speaker, be it on the Left or Right, I do not care, they all make the same point as the set in a circular way around the table.

The president gives others the floor so that the same recorded words can be given, always the same opinions, and many times with the same gestures, the speech always paired with the phrase "our honored dead." The use of "our" infuriates me, it's an ownership title over the dead. I ask for the floor:

"Sir Mayor, colleagues, of course you are aware that among the Greeks who were executed at the range there were some revolutionaries and highwaymen[25]. I kindly ask that we make sure to lay a wreath in their memory." Naturally, they remove me from the floor, but I try to continue, they shut my mouth, others cuss me out, someone from the audience calls me profane.

---

25. *Translator's note: Chakkas uses the word "saltadóri," which specifically references Greek resistance fighters who pillaged German tanks and vehicles during the occupation.*

I think about those tough kids whose council member was hunger and whose ideal was the reserve. They reached the moat all on their own without hope that the party would hold a memorial for them, without any subsequent justice. And how can you support them in their loneliness? The others had people to cry over them, hundreds of wreaths, slogans, songs and poems. The others, most of them, had a place to lean on, a vision, a cause that they believed moved forward, regardless of whether or not it was also scrapped in the end, their descendants would yell out the names of the fallen at the demonstrations. On which ideas can the bandit lean on?

"I jumped on top of the car and sliced the hood open using my knife. The others ran behind me so that I could toss them the stolen goods. That is when I saw the Germans waiting for me with their pistols. I could have jumped back down anyway, but I thought to myself that I'd be putting the others running behind the car in danger. I let go and they caught me in their arms. I thought that it would be just like last time: Averof, a tree that cut down years[26]. They sent me to Chaidári. Now I walk into the pen toward the moat, the walking path, and the only thing I can think about is to avoid stepping on the long grass. I did not do any great deeds in my life, I never thought about ideas and stuff

26. Translator's note: Averof prison, active between 1892-1971. Also a possible reference to the tree in the prison courtyard mentioned in "Of My Own Free Will."

like that, the only thing I can avoid doing in these last moments is harming the grass."

We were received by the secretary of the Shooting Range Heritage Association, I did not retain his name, but I can pick him out of a thousand people, he is thin, probably short and with silvery hair. He received us near the human dummies, a thirty meter shooting range, and he was screaming "which memorial?", and made many gestures, his neck was fragile, particularly the moment when he said "so if the roof of your house collapses and kills ten or twelve people, will their relatives require a memorial to be held in your house every year?", his little neck was begging to be strangled, so, the moment he said those words, you could place your thumb there and squeeze until his voice stopped coming out of his throat. Or you could put him in the pen with the dummies, in the thirty meter shooting range, yelling "hide, scumbag" at him, and aim somewhere near his feet, pull the trigger so that the bullets ricochet off of the dummies, "dance and don't be afraid, I will go back to your family so that they can have a memorial for you every year even if it's an accident, where can I find the roof at this uncovered area?"

Just wait and see, they will turn this place into plots of land—six meters in width and twelve in depth each, just enough so that it is divided evenly. Everyone will agree about the plots, the Right, Left, and Center, despite their differences, their common denominator being their "acreage."

The "Refugees" will move in first regardless of which administration they belong to. Then, "Worker's Housing" will join the dance so that they can accommodate workers. The state will then hand out keys. Of course, some school will also be built, but without a yard, and the kids will have recess out on the street.

I don't know if in the end the little forest will be saved. The right thing would be to exterminate it too so that it doesn't exist for busts, to rule out any possibility of heroes, cenotaphs, and candles. Of course, the land behind the cemetery will never be developed. On the contrary, they will decorate and beautify it all of the time. Lately they've even erected a large concrete cross so that it can serve as a reminder of the "well," the Battle of Meligalás. You look around but don't find a well, you don't even find a puddle. And anyway, this space will slowly acquire a new name from the frequent memorial services and the schools visiting to lay wreaths, and the future visitor will think that maybe somewhere nearby there was a "well" that was filled with the corpses of nationalists. There is a possibility that the name "Shooting Range" will remain, but it will become neutral, it will not hold any significant meaning, it will be like Syntagma square, it will remind people of those loafers who shoot at paper targets, at clay plates and pigeons. They would never shoot at people. During the German occupation? When did such a thing ever happen?